BLIND LOVE

A Novel By
Dee Cohoon-Madore

DEELIGHTFUL READING

Copyright 2021
Self-published by:
Dee Cohoon-Madore Self-Publishing
Digby, NS, Canada

Visit DEELIGHTFUL READING on the web at
http://deelightfulreading.com
e-mail: dee@deelightfulreading.com

All rights reserved. No part of this book may be reproduced or transmitted in any form or by any means, electronic or mechanical, including photocopying, recording or by any information storage and retrieval system, without the written permission of the author, except where permitted by law.

The novel Blind Love is fictional. Any similarity to actual persons, either living or dead, is entirely coincidental.

About the Author

Dee, a vivacious young senior, lives in Digby with her husband, Jim. Home is where she escapes into endless hours of writing.

Dee (known then as Darlene), born the fifth of ten children, grew up in a relatively poor family in a rural Nova Scotia community. Coming from a seriously  dysfunctional family made her childhood an unhappy place. Her parents separated when she was eight years old, leaving her mother with a brood of kids to raise independently. Moving became the norm, having no place to call 'home' for any great length of time. She has memories of her mother wrapping dishes in old newspapers and packing them into a barrel: sparse household furnishings and the bare essentials made for a hasty move in those days. Life was far from easy for the Cohoon family.

At twenty, she married her childhood sweetheart and moved to Toronto for several years. Although the marriage could have been a good one, it only lasted for seven years, but it brought her two beautiful children. It seemed as if she had come full circle since now being a single mom. But despite living on a shoestring budget, she proudly saw both her children graduate from high school to begin new lives and careers of their own.

The empty nest situation allowed Dee the opportunity to focus on furthering her own education. With an entrepreneurial spirit, she formed a company and operated a successful business for several years. It was during these years that she met her future husband.

After remarrying, she began to seriously focus on her writing. She had accumulated notebooks and scraps of writings, but nothing really materialized until she finished her first novel, 'Gifted' in 2008. Her second book, 'Tidbits, Tips & Treasures,' is a self-help book meant to have something for everyone. 'Gypsy Heart,' a semi-autobiographical, took on a more personal side. There has been a bit of a break since publishing her last book, 'The Grand Manor,' but hopefully, the wait for 'Blind Love' will have been worth it for her readers.

All of Dee's books are available on her website, at deelightfulreading.com.

She hopes you will let her know your thoughts by leaving a comment on her website after settling in with any of her novels. She reads and personally replies to every bit of correspondence so, don't be shy. She would love to hear from you.

Dedicated to:

My God, He is my source of words beyond my understanding. He gave me the gift of words and enabled me to turn them into stories for my readers to enjoy and hopefully relate to.

My thoughts, ideas and notions were inspired by Him, and without His constant presence in my life, this book would not exist.

His guidance and everlasting love have led me to this place of Peace, Tranquility, and Creativity I now enjoy.

This book is also dedicated to my sister Debbie who passed away in March 2019, at 63.

Debbie dedicated an enormous part of her life to caring for seniors in her home at Cliff Haven Manor. I want to honour her in this book, and I know how she would have enjoyed reading it and getting lost in the words of my story at Cliff Haven Castle. We once were five (sisters), and now we are four, and we miss you every day.

Acknowledgements

I wish to thank my daughter, Tara, for taking the time out of her busy military and personal life and offering to be my beta reader. Without her time and patience, this book would not have made it to this timeline.

Thank you to the readers for your continued support and encouragement. Without it, there would be no determination or desire to put stories together.

I wish to extend a sincere and heartfelt thank you to Cedar Springs, my publisher and web designer, for always being there for me. For tirelessly giving time and advice and for being my 'go-to guy.' Without you, this book would not have made it to print.

Lastly, to my dedicated readers, thank you for your patience, your gracious comments on my website and most especially, for requesting to be on the list for future book releases. Oh, and just so you know, Keeping Secrets is in the editing stage and will soon be ready to launch.

This is for my friend, mentor, and pen pal for more than 30 years.

My life consists of two kinds of Time
The Time when I am with you
And the Time when I am waiting
To be with you again
G.A.Z.

Everyone has their own path. Walk yours with integrity and wish all others peace on their journey. When your paths merge, rejoice for their presence in your life. When the paths are separated, return to the wholeness of yourself, give thanks for the footprints left on your soul, and embrace the time to journey on your own.

Author Unknown

Sharing a book is an encouragement to read. Encouraging others to purchase a book is an encouragement to the author.

From the Author

Words, thoughts, ideas, images, and dreams send me scrambling for a pencil and a notepad. When I am nestled down in bed for the night, they come to me, and my mind goes off in a million different directions. I reach out into the darkness to turn on my bedside lamp and pull open the drawer where my stash of paper and several mechanical pencils live until I need them. I jot down what seems like a novel idea, and several pages later, I pull up my blankets and turn off the light.

Once this book takes flight, I have three others waiting for my attention. This is not to mention the titles I have written in a notebook for future books if I should live long enough to finish them all.

I hope you enjoy this latest story, and I ask that you send me your comment, good or bad, I can take it. Feedback feeds my soul, inspires me, and spurs me on to continue bringing my books to you.

You can contact me through my website, www.delightfulreading.com or email dee@cedarsprings.cc, and your comment will be added to the comment section on the site.

BLIND LOVE

A Novel By
Dee Cohoon-Madore

1
Isabella's story

Pregnant at fifteen and still in high school, Isabella's parents thought she should marry the baby's father. She was only a child herself and felt she was too young for such a lifelong commitment to a boy who had no use for her anymore. So, she lied and said she didn't know who the father was. Refusing to name the boy was a relief to her since marriage was the last thing on her mind. By lying to her parents, they would not have anyone, in particular, to hunt down and force them into marriage. Isabella knew that it was a mistake in the first place, and when he filled her head with lies and then tossed her aside, she just wanted to forget about him entirely.

Since putting them in such a position, her parents said they'd have to think about their options for Isabella and her unborn child. Those were scary words for a young girl to hear, so Isabella began thinking of ways that could, hopefully, help her raise her baby alone. She was nervous and scared as she waited for her parents to come up with their solution, so she began, secretly, making plans of her own. It was her future they were planning out, and Isabella refused to leave it up to her parents. She'd gotten herself into this mess, so now she had to come up with a plan to fix it without their help.

For days, she surreptitiously searched the newspaper ads for a job. But every day, it carried the same ads until finally, a new lot of ads were listed. While scanning through them, she'd come across an interesting write-up for a housekeeper. 'This might be perfect,' she thought, "it wouldn't be such a hard job. After all, I help out around here, so there wouldn't be anything too strenuous for now.'

Jotting down the information, she stuffed the paper into her pocket. She quietly folded the newspaper back to its original condition. She had saved a few pieces of change, so with them in her pocket and the address from the paper, she silently left the house and scurried downtown to use a payphone. She prayed that she'd be the first to apply for the job since she needed one so badly.

"Hello?" he said, "how may I direct your call?"

"I'm calling about the ad in this morning's newspaper," she told the man who'd answered the phone.

"I see, you're our first applicant. When can you come for an interview?" he asked.

"I am available now if it's convenient," she said nervously.

"Yes, yes," he said, "please come then. Do you have directions?"

"Yes, I have them," she reassured him, "I am on foot, so I am hoping to be there within the hour."

Hanging up the phone, she was relieved that she was the first caller. Now, if only she could get there without any delays, she'd be quite satisfied.

***

It was a longer walk than she thought. From downtown to the countryside was a good hike, but Isabella kept a steady pace until she came to the address. She could hardly believe the tiresome walk up the long and winding driveway. It took almost as long to walk its distance as it did to walk from town. Tired and hot, she slipped off her coat and folded it over her arm and finished the walk. She couldn't believe her eyes when she looked up from the ground and saw what was spread out at the top of the driveway. She thought she must have jotted down the wrong numbers to the civic address. But since she's come this far, she thought she might as well finish. It was one of the grandest castles that she'd only heard about but never had the opportunity to see. It was breathtakingly beautiful yet spooky, spooky but intriguing, grand and lovely all at the same time. Walking up the few steps and taking a deep breath, she lifted the heavy doorknocker of the enormous and elaborate door.

Knocking several times, she stood back and waited, and when the door opened, it was as if time had stood still for them. She gazed into the eyes of an impeccably dressed young and handsome fellow whom she estimated to be somewhere in his early to mid twenty's. He had a full head of dark brown wavy hair, neatly combed to perfection. Large and dreamy brown eyes that looked like pools of dark and yummy chocolate and their stunned silence spoke volumes. His full and perfectly shaped lips stretched out into a full and welcoming grin. He was wearing navy blue dress pants and a red plaid shirt with a navy vee-neck sweater over top and expensive-looking dockers on his feet. He stood about a head taller than her at about five-eight.

After a brief scan up and down his frame, her thoughts came back to the reason she was there.

Straightening her shoulders and her head held high, she smiled and said in a voice as grown-up as what she could muster, "I am Isabella Merrick, and I am here for the job interview."

"Are you? Are you indeed?" he said. Stepping aside, he swooped his hand and bowed at the waist for her to enter. "Please, do come in then," he said with a smile and straightened up when she passed him. His actions indicated that he was a jovial, young and ambitious butler.

It was the grandest place she'd ever been in or had ever seen. It felt as if she'd stepped into a fairytale storybook as she crossed the threshold and into a grand castle. Looking around, she could hardly believe she was actually inside one of the most gorgeous and most magnificent of places in all of Kanyon Cliffs. Her eyes followed a beautiful and endlessly winding staircase that went up and up into… who knows where… but beyond that of which she could see from where she stood. The ceiling went straight up to somewhere on the second floor. Lush floor-to-ceiling powder blue velvet drapes adorned the windows, which filled up most of the walls and were tied back to receive the natural light. On the floors lay carpets that were thick, plush, and soft beneath her feet. They were colourful and vibrant, and she thought perhaps they were most likely specially ordered from a foreign country and much too beautiful for a foyer. He stood with his heels together and his hands clasped behind his back, giving her enough time to absorb the opulence of the enormous entry. Leading the way, she followed him into a huge but comfortable room that could have been a den, a library or a drawing-room. She didn't know which. A cozy fire crackled in the fireplace that spoke comfort and relaxation. She wasn't sure if she was standing with a butler, a footman, or another staff member.

"May I take your coat, Miss Merrick?" he asked.

"Please, call me Isabella," she said, raising her arm for him to remove the coat.

'So, he's a butler then,' she thought. He laid her coat across the back of a chair. At the same time, she was preoccupied with taking in the magnificence of this beautifully decorated room.

He took the opportunity to check her out while she was familiarizing herself with the room. She glanced upwards to the sparkling and elegant crystal chandelier. She then scanned the walls at the enormous works of art that were on display. She was amazed at the many pieces of matching furniture that could only belong in this room. Each sitting area had its own small and round tea table close at hand for convenience's sake.

On the other hand, he had never, in his lifetime, seen anyone quite this lovely in all of his travels, including most parts of the world. When there was nothing left to amuse him, he'd settled down here at Cliff Haven Castle. At this moment he was happy that travelling had become boring and had brought him back home. He was all but ogling as she found delight in what she was seeing.

He had a few delightful moments of his own as he gazed at her hair that flowed down her back like wild sun-streaked wheat and settled at the halfway point at her back. She had wide and innocent blue-green eyes, with naturally long and curled eyelashes. He thought that he'd have no problem at all getting lost in those gorgeous eyes if he wasn't already. Those delightfully full and sensual lips and oval face drew this package altogether. He considered her to be 'well built' for such a young girl. She had curves in all the right places and with the smile of an angel. Standing next to her, she was nearly a match to him in height. He was totally in awe of this young lady. Shaking the image from his mind and finding his manners, "Please, sit down," he said, moving his hand towards one of several sofas.

"I think I've made a terrible mistake," Isabella confessed as she lifted her fingertips to her lips.

"Oh? Whatever do you mean?" he asked, furrowing his brow.

"This is not what I expected for a job as a housekeeper," she said, "I have to be honest with you, sir. I couldn't possibly keep this place clean," she admitted with a wave of her hand. "I thought I was answering an ad for a housekeeper, not a castle keeper. I wouldn't do the job justice, I'm afraid. Do you have any other positions available?" she asked, trying not to sound desperate.

He could have corrected her immediately to explain that the entire house was not her job alone but that she would have been only one of the many hires. But he wanted to know more, and if he had to create a job for her, then so be it! "Actually, I do," he said, giving pause to his answer. "I'm looking for a personal secretary to assist with the daily running of the place," he lied. 'Sampson would have an absolute fit if he thought he had to share his job with a new hire,' he smiled secretly at the thought.

Isabella smiled at the word secretary, which he pronounced sec-ra-tree. 'He was British alright,' she thought, 'and oh... soooo handsome!'

"Do you have any experience in that department?" he asked, bringing them both back into the conversation.

"I... don't," she said honestly, shaking her head as she spoke, "but I could learn," she said, nodding her head eagerly. "If you could take the time to show me, I'm sure I could prove my worth." Holding her breath, she waited for him to answer. She knew that cleaning this big castle, mansion or ark, would be too much once her situation became more delicate. Not to mention what would happen once her tummy started to grow. She knew if she could land a job soon and hide the pregnancy long enough, it would give her time to save a few dollars to tide her over, so she could start over somewhere else.

"You have no experience at all, eh?" he asked curiously. "Not even a tiny bit of bookkeeping, accounting, organizing, etcetera, etcetera," he said, rolling his hand around in a small circle.

"The only experience I have is what I've learned at school. Balancing a bank book, typing, making schedules... you know..." she said, flipping her hand, "basic office stuff," she said nervously.

Relieved to hear that, "So you do have some experience," he said, leaning forward with interest. "Jolly good! Now we're getting somewhere..., let me show you around the office then," he said with a broad and satisfied grin. 'Now,' he thought, as Sampson came to mind, 'he wouldn't have to justify his hiring her. 'Not that he owed an explanation to anyone,' he thought, 'but Sampson did run a tight and efficient ship. Just the same, though, he could not let this beauty just up and walk out the door. That would be absurd!'

Getting up from her seat, she followed him into a neat and tidy office. Everything was brown wood, hardwood floors, wainscoting on the walls and then something similar to wood paneling from the wainscoting to the high ceiling. It was rather drab, but if she got the job, then she'd cope with its decor.

"We have a full staff that takes care of the entire estate, and each one likely has a different salary, which payroll is part of the job. I can teach you how to do that. We have a full-time accountant, so we only have to do enough to satisfy him," he said, winking at her jokingly. "Are you interested at all in helping me out?" he said, looking at her with hope in his eyes.

"May I ask a question first?" she said directly.

"Of course, you may," he said, admiring her honesty.

"Is there a place nearby that provides room and board?" she asked.

"Room and board?" he questioned, pulling his neck in and furrowing his brow, "what a ghastly thought. Aren't you a bit young to be out on your own?" he asked with concern, "don't you have parents?"

"I do, but complications are forcing me to leave home. I must find a job and take care of myself and look for a place to live. I can't afford an apartment," she said honestly, "so a rooming house will have to do for now."

Mortified, he couldn't believe what he was hearing. "Do you mind if I ask why you are out on your own?" he said, with a look of concern.

Shifting her eyes and wringing her fingers for several seconds, she thought her chances of working here would be over. She decided that honesty was the best policy, and it was 'do or die' at the moment. "I... um... I'm... pregnant, and I don't know what my parents have planned for my baby, so I want to raise it on my own."

Mellowing, he was in awe of this beautiful woman-child, who was trusting him with such a personal secret. He knew that Isabella could have easily told him any lie possible. Still, when he asked her the question, she barely hesitated to answer him.

"Well, that sheds a different light on things, now doesn't it?" he said, realizing now why she couldn't possibly housekeep. He noticed her shoulders drop in defeat, and she struggled to keep her face from giving in to crying. Pressing her lips together tightly for several seconds, she said, "I see, well, thank you for seeing me. I'll show myself out."

"Excuse me?" he said, creasing his brow.

"I'll be going now," she said, "I suppose there aren't many places that will take in a pregnant schoolgirl," she said truthfully. "Going back home to face the plan that my parents have cooked up for me seems like my only option."

"Umm... no," he said, shaking his head, "you don't understand. I want to hire you, and I want to offer you a room here. It comes with the job anyway. All the workers stay here if they choose to. I won't put you upstairs in the maid's quarters, though, but directly through here," he said, pointing to a side door, "is a spacious bedroom that would be quite fitting for you. Here, let me show you," he said, putting his hand on her back and slightly pushing her towards the door. Leaning past her, he turned the doorknob and pushed the door open. In his heart of hearts, he hoped that she'd like it and agree to stay.

Isabella was stunned. Her feet wouldn't move, so he pressed his palm against her back to get her started. Stepping inside, she put her hands up to her face and looked around at the magnificence of the room. It also had floor-to-ceiling windows with soft yellow draperies. And garden doors led out to a cobblestone path lined with lush bushes, green trees, colourful and picture-perfect flower gardens. Inside, the room had everything mentionable, including an ensuite bathroom. The old four-poster king-size bed sat between two enormous windows. It was directly across from the garden doors, and white silk tulle hung from the posters of the bed, forming a canape. A soft, pale blue comforter covered the bed, and there were mounds of colourful yellow accent pillows. A tall and wide mahogany armoire filled up most of one wall. It was every girl's dream bedroom and something straight out of a 'Better Homes' magazine.

"Seriously?" she gushed, still in awe of his generous offer. "Do I pay for this out of my wages? It would surely beat a lonely room and board establishment."

"There is no charge if you accept the job. We provide rooms for all the staff. How else would we possibly fill all of these rooms?" he said, waving a hand around and smiling broadly. "And," he added, "this door, right here," he pointed, "leads out into the hall from where we came into the office." He waited for her to absorb the information and get her bearings. "Well...? Do you accept my offer?" he said with his heart on his sleeve. Before she had a chance to answer, he spoke again. "You know, later on, there is ample room in here for a crib," he said, pointing to several locations and hoped that she'd see what he'd envisioned. "And, after that," he went on, "we have a full-time nanny on staff as well." He stopped there, thinking he's said enough, which most of it was out of pure desperation.

Looking at him for several seconds, she put the back of her hand to her lips and nodded her head. Relief flowed through him, and he couldn't stop himself from going over to her. It wasn't very professional of him, but he lifted her off the floor and spun her around a couple of times before setting her back down. "Welcome to my home, Miss Isabella."

"Your... home?" she asked. "You didn't introduce yourself when you let me in. Who are you? We've been chatting about a job, but I don't even know your name. I thought you were the butler!" she said.

"Oh," he said, pulling his neck in, surprised that he could have so rudely overlooked that. He was desperate to convince Isabella to stay that he'd forgotten about introducing himself. "I'm so sorry! How terribly rude of me, I am Lord Charles Wellington III, but you can call me Charlie," he said, faking a bow. "When would you prefer to start your new job?" he asked.

"Lord...? I'll be working for a... a... Lord...?" she fumbled the words bringing him to laughter.

"Only because my father was one," he joked and flipped his hand like it was no big deal.

A sense of peace flowed through her as she realized that he had been a kind and loving person from the moment he opened the front door at her knock.

"So, if you have staff, why did you answer the door?" she asked curiously.

"Well, I must confess," he said with a sheepish grin. "I was watching as you were walking up the lane, so I sent the butler on an errand so I could greet you personally. Was that rude of me?" he asked.

"Maybe a little," she giggled. Pondering a thought, she said, "If I had known I was able to start today, I would have brought a bag."

He noticed that she was uncomfortable about something, and he couldn't help but ask. "Can I help you with anything? A car perhaps, to go and fetch your things?" he asked with concern. He was already a goner over this woman, and he knew he'd do absolutely anything for her.

"I don't actually want to go back home," she said adamantly.

"Why ever not?" he exclaimed.

"My parents might insist that I stay there, and I don't want to," she said firmly.

"Then you won't!" he said just as firmly.

"But I have no clothes!" she laughed.

He adored her genuine laugh, and he thought that he might love her already.

"We can fix that!" he said, giving his fingers a quick snap.

"How can you fix my lack of clothing?" she said, laughing again, "are you also a magician?"

"In this case, I'll say yes, so come with me," he insisted and grabbed her hand and walked quickly through the house and up the elegant staircase to the second floor. There were endless doors on both sides of the hall, but he seemed to know exactly where to go. He pulled a key from his pocket and unlocked the door. Charlie unlocked the door and swung it open to expose a beautiful frilly room that seemed fit for any queen.

"What is this?" she exclaimed as her mouth hung open in surprise.

"It was my sister's room, and you can have anything you want from in here," he said and waved his hand around the room, smiling broadly.

"I can't do that. What would she say?"

"Nothing," he said, widening his eyes, "she left and has never returned, and her room is the same as when she left it, so it's all yours now."

"Where is she?" Isabella asked.

"She went traipsing off to some foreign country and married a... a king... or... something or other," he joked, making swirly hand gestures into the air. He swung open the doors to an enormous armoire with rows and rows of clothes on hangers, several drawers and shelving filled with every incidental possible.

"Take whatever you'll need for a couple of days, and I'll leave the key in the office, on a hook, and you can transfer everything downstairs at your leisure. Does this solve your problem?" he joked and lifted his nose in the air like a snob.

"I believe it does, Charlie. I will make my choices, in private, a bit later if you don't mind," she smiled shyly while thinking about picking out underwear in his presence.

"Not at all," he said, leading the way out and down the hall, and they sashayed down the grand staircase and back to the den, library or drawing-room. She still wasn't sure which yet.

"May I call you Bella?" he asked, raising his eyebrows in question.

"You would be the first, but yes, I guess it would be OK," she said, "I have always been called Isabella. So, new home, new job, new life and a new name, I think it's perfect."

"It is absolutely perfect," he said, stepping closer to her. Reaching out his hands, she took them, and he said, "I think you are rather perfect too, Miss Bella."

"I am jail bait," she teased, even though she knew he was serious. She wasn't about to take the bait off the hook just yet. She was already dealing with one problem because of stupidity. She wasn't about to jump into the deep end again, not yet anyway. "I am not yet sixteen, pregnant and a run-away. What are we going to do if the police show up here looking for me?"

"Oh! Well, that's a rather ominous picture," he said. "How did you get here?" he asked curiously.

"My only option, I walked," she said, pointing to her sad-looking shoes, "I have no money for a cab or bus fare," she admitted, hunching her shoulders.

"Did you meet anyone along the way? Or did anyone offer you a ride?" he asked.

"Actually, no, it's pretty quiet and isolated out here away from town," she said.

"Well, if the police arrive, we'll deal with it then. When are you turning sixteen?" Charlie asked.

"Not for a month," she offered.

"I will give the staff strict instructions for the utmost discretion, and we'll wait it out together. Once you've reached sixteen, then your life is your own," he pointed out. But what he didn't say was, by then, she'd be old enough to be his Lady Isabella of Cliff Haven Castle.

"Bella, would you like some tea or something?" he asked, flipping his hand towards her and reaching for a signal button on the wall. Pausing his finger in mid-air near the switch, he waited for her to answer.

"I would like some tea, please," she answered.

"Wonderful," he said and pressed the button.

"Yes, sir, what can I get for you?" came a voice over a speaker. Isabella was impressed with the setup they had for communication.

"Sampson, tea for two, please, in the west library," but he paused the conversation to ask, "Bella, are you hungry?"

'Ah, the west library,' she said, noting his instructions to Sampson, whoever that was. "Yes, Charlie, I am starved, actually," she admitted.

"Sampson? Just bring a luncheon for two, with tea, thank you!" he said in a sing-songy voice that made her giggle. Letting go of the button, Charlie came directly over to Bella and sat beside her, not across from her as she'd expected, but she was thrilled nonetheless. He was the kindest and most gracious person that she'd ever met. He was also witty and fun to be around.

She had been at the house for three hours, but it seemed as if it were only ten minutes. It was as if they'd known each other for years. They were comfortable in each other's presence, and there was nothing but honesty and trust between them. It had all the makings for the perfect relationship.

2
Sweet Sixteen

Waking up early on the morning of her birthday, Isabella laid in bed. She thought about how fortunate she'd been to come across Charlie's ad. Looking around the room that she had claimed as her own, she still couldn't believe that she lived in a castle and worked for a handsome Lord. She tried to wrap her head around it all when a tap, tap came on her door. Sitting up, she pulled the covers up in front of her. Before she had a chance to ask who it was, a voice came from the other side of the door.

"Bella? May I come in, please?"

It was Charlie, and she was concerned that something had happened to bring him to her door.

"Yes, come in!" she said.

Opening the door, he entered the room, carrying a breakfast tray. It was shoulder high and on the tips of his fingers on one hand and waved the room with the other as if he was making a grand entrance. Bella smiled as she watched him acting out his butler routine. He was such a character.

"Happy Birthday, Bella," he said with a big bright grin on his face.

"Charlie, you remembered!"

"Of course, Darling Bella, I remembered," he said with a happy grin.

She couldn't pretend she didn't like the word 'darling' that he'd slipped into his words, and she looked at him shyly.

"I thought perhaps the police had found me," she said, looking worried.

"Not to worry, my darling, it's just me, your humble servant," he teased, placing the tray across her lap and taking care not to touch anything on her person. Not that he hadn't thought about doing just that for the past month, but he'd had his naughty thoughts tucked away for now.

"Breakfast in bed! A first for me!" she said, eyeing the tray as he adjusted it in front of her. "It looks yummy!"

He'd remembered to place a linen napkin on the tray for her, with an egg sitting in an egg cup, toast accompanied with a crystal bowl of strawberry jam and a glass of cold milk. 'Who was she kidding? It was the kitchen staff who'd done the tray,' she thought, but it seemed that he wanted to take the credit. "Thank you, Charlie. I feel so spoiled."

"You are very welcome, my Darling," he said, smiling. He couldn't help but notice how beautiful she looked in the morning. Clean washed face, her lovely hair pulled to one side in a braid that hung down over her right breast, and she always had a smile for him.

Bella, on the other hand, gobbled up the attention that Charlie was giving her. Never, in her sixteen years, has anyone been this kind to her. He pulled up a chair at her bedside and insisted that she go ahead and eat, and he'd keep her company for her birthday breakfast.

"I can't possibly allow you to eat alone on your birthday," he said, smiling at her with that grin she was ever so familiar with and looked forward to seeing.

"Well, I can't possibly eat with you staring at me!" she said, loving that he'd preferred to sit with her in her room rather than in the dining room.

"Nonsense!" he said, waving at the tray, "eat up!"

"Have you eaten?" she asked.

"No, not yet, but I will, later, this is your time," he said, looking at her.

"Eat with me then!" she said, moving the tray closer to him.

Reaching for a piece of toast, he picked up the jam spoon, dipped it in the jar, and dropped it on top of the toast. Picking up the knife, he spread the jam across it and leaned back in the chair, holding the toast between his fingers.

"We've managed to escape any police investigations," he said, putting on another grin for her, and biting into the toast. "Perhaps you left no clue when you disappeared," he added, flipping his hands in the air as if it were magic.

Isabella thought that this castle would be the last place they'd look if anyone were looking for her.

"Or... maybe nobody cared that I was gone," she said, looking at him sideways. "Either way, I don't care," she admitted, "I feel safer now that I've turned sixteen today, and legally, I am free to come and go as I please. Thank you, Charlie, for your help and for giving me a job and shelter. I truly don't know where I'd be if I hadn't seen your ad."

"I'm glad you're here, Bella. Now eat your breakfast. We must keep you healthy."

When he spoke to her, he never mentioned her pregnancy or that she was eating for two now, as the saying goes. It was always just about her. It caused her some concern, but it was early yet, and she was beginning to round out. Her belly was no longer as flat as a pancake, and her breasts were fuller and more tender.

Charlie couldn't help but notice the fullness of her breasts since the bedding was lying at her waist, just below them. His fingertips tingled at the thought of touching them and her, but he had to wait for the proper time. She'd only been with him for a month, and it had been challenging to keep his hands off a fifteen-year-old girl. He had never mistaken her friendly gratitude for anything more than what it was.

Working closely with her in the office gave him many heated moments that caused him to make excuses to step away for a few minutes. He'd step out into the hall and take several deep breaths and wait for his heartbeat to settle down before going back in. He'd told himself honestly that he could have done the office work with his eyes closed, but when she showed up at his door, there was no way he was letting her leave.

Bella's entire month in hiding, he barely left the house so she wouldn't feel alone or abandoned in this huge place. Besides, there was no place that he'd rather have been than next to her. They'd spend time walking in the gardens on nice days and in the library, reading books, magazines, and newspapers on cold or rainy days. She'd even learned to knit from a how-to instruction booklet that had been tucked away in a magazine. She'd asked Charlie if someone from the kitchen could bring her some yarn and needles from one of their trips to town. She'd given him money that she'd received from her job, and he took it to the kitchen, along with the pattern and asked one of the maids for her assistance. It took her several frustrating attempts to learn how to cast on stitches and follow a pattern, but she did it. On those rainy or cool days and evenings enjoying the fireplace, she finished a baby sweater, a bonnet and a pair of booties. She was certain her baby was a boy, so she'd deliberately chosen blue yarn.

3

Isabella had made several trips upstairs to the 'frilly room' and picked out clothes that would fit her as her body changed shape. There were closets filled with every possible style. She chose loose outfits for this stage, and there were many more choices. It was as if she had her very own clothing store right there in the castle.

Expanding, even more, Isabella took another trip upstairs to search for something more comfortable and loose. Before she got to the armoire, she saw several beautiful smocks laid out perfectly on the bed. Holding one up against her shoulders, she looked in the full-length mirror and turned this way and that to get a good look when she was interrupted.

"I hope they fit and that you like them," Charlie said, leaning against the door frame. Lowering the hanger, she had to admit that he looked quite sexy standing there, his arms folded across his chest. He had one foot crossed over the other and that grin... oh, how she loved that grin.

"Charlie, you didn't ha..."

"I wanted to," he said, cutting her words off. He tilted his head, and she saw it in his eyes. It had been there all along, but this time she allowed herself to see it. Charlie was not a player, like the boys at school, and she had to let that go and live in the moment. A smile dropped from her face as she realized what was happening.

Pushing off the door frame, he stood and waited. The hanger slipped from Isabella's fingers, and as it hit the floor, she slowly stepped over it and moved towards him. "Charlie," she said softly.

"Bella," he whispered.

Stepping away from the doorway and into the room, he reached for her. Spreading her arms out to him, he gathered her up into a loving embrace. "My Darling Bella, I've wanted this for so long," he said, whispered into her neck.

"I think I have too, Charlie, but I had to be sure."

Pulling slightly apart, they looked into each other's eyes. Dropping her eyes to Charlie's lips, she saw them part as he waited for her to make the next move. If there were to be 'a next move,' then it would be hers to make.

Lifting her head slowly and parting her lips, she invited him in. Covering her lips with his, their excitement and passion soared. As he devoured her with his mouth, he pressed her close to him. He'd waited for this moment for months, but it had been worth it.

"Charlie, I never dared to hope that you'd ever want me. I'm not worthy of you, especially since I am with child, I would never ask you to ...,"

"To what?" he asked, "be a father to your child? Make a home for an innocent baby?" he added. "You can bet that I want all of those things!" he said, spreading his arms out and then resting them on her shoulders.

"Wait! What!? Charlie?" she asked in shock. "Whatever are you saying?"

"Marry me, Bella, be my wife, and we can raise this child as our own," he said. "Who would be the wiser? You came here as a single girl; we fell in love and got married. Who can argue that?" he said, shrugging his shoulders.

"I... I... don't know what to say!" Bella sputtered.

"Then say yes, Bella and be the Lady of Cliff Haven Castle," he said, spreading his hands apart, dramatically, as if displaying her to the entire world. Seeing the look of surprise on her face, he bent slowly and touched his lips to hers. Moving in closer, he deepened his kiss, and raising her arms, she put them around his back and pulled him tighter.

"Oh, Charlie," she breathed, "I think I've loved you from the moment you answered my knock, but I thought perhaps that I was only being silly. How could I love someone at first sight?"

"You can, and I did, Bella," he whispered, "from the moment I opened the door, probably even while watching you walk up the driveway. I love you, my Darling, from the moment I saw you. Marry me, Bella."

"Are you sure, Charlie? What about the staff?" she asked.

"It's not them I'm worried about at the moment, Bella. I'm asking you and only you, to marry me," he said softly. "It has nothing to do with them."

"I will, Charlie," she said, taking his face in her hands and spreading a smile across her face, "I will marry you!"

4

Isabella Merrick and Lord Charles Wellington, III, were married at Cliff Haven Castle. The staff had decorated the enormous foyer with large pots of colourful flowers from the gardens and trailed them down the banister.

She had refused Charlie's offer to purchase a wedding gown when his sister had many beautiful unworn dresses in her closet. Olivia, a lady's maid, helped Bella chose a pale pink strapless full-length gown. It clung to her body to the waist then flowed out in layers of silk with a full hooped crinoline and a satin petticoat. At the top of her head, Olivia helped her place a diamond tiara. A veil attached to the tiara flowed down her back and trailed to the floor behind her. She chose a delicate pair of pink ballerina slippers, and her floor-length gown hid them perfectly. She didn't want to wear heels and seem taller than she was. She felt that she and Charlie looked great together without deliberately towering over him.

Isabella glided down the staircase. She held her head high and her shoulders straight while holding a handmade bouquet in front of her at tummy height. It was made of large white roses, tiny pink rose buds and trails of greenery.

In Charlies's eyes, there was no one more beautiful than this vision coming down the stairs with eyes only for him. He'd loved this gorgeous creature from the moment he first laid his eyes upon her. This day only made him love her that much more.

Once they repeated their vows and heard toasts from those who felt the need to give one, Charlie was ready for some long-awaited, alone time with his bride. As the staff celebrated, Charles and Isabella slipped off to the rear of the house. They ran excitedly up the back staircase to his room. Charlie swooped her up in his arms and carried her over the threshold and into their bedroom suite. Fresh rose petals were spread across the room and up onto the bed. Newly cut flowers were arranged in vases and sat on the tables, and adorned the bedposts leaving a sensational fragrance throughout the room.

Laying Isabella down on a literal bed of rose petals, he felt as if he was the luckiest man alive.

"I love you, my sweet Bella," he whispered as he traced her with his eyes, unable to believe this beauty belonged to him.

Sitting up, Bella slipped off the bed. Reaching up, she lifted the tiara from her hair and laid it at the foot of the bed. Turning her back to Charlie, she pulled her hair to one side. Without words, he unzipped her dress, slipped it off her shoulders, and it dropped at her waist. Leaning her head back against him, he slipped his hands around her front. Opening his fingers, he encircled her slightly swollen breast and pressed his lips against the side of her neck. Her skin felt like velvet against his palms. She placed her hands over his and pressed his hands into a squeeze. His excitement grew as she moaned, and he felt the rise and fall of her chest against his touch when her breathing changed.

"Bella, my darling," he whispered at the back of her neck.

Stepping out of the mound of material at her feet, she stood before him in just a pair of frilly panties. Reaching out for her, she stepped into the circle of his arms and wrapped herself around him. Picking up his sexy young bride, he laid her on top of their bed of rose petals. Charlie and Isabella were the only two people in the world until they chose otherwise.

✶✶✶

Life at the castle met with very few challenges. Isabella and Charlie welcomed their son, Logan, into the world. Charlie insisted that their baby boy, Charles Logan Merrick Wellington, was written on his birth certificate. In the Wellington family bible, Logan was one of the last Wellington's to be entered until, of course, if Logan were to have a son or daughter.

Although he wasn't blood kin to Charlie, only he and Isabella and Logan, in time, were privy to that information.

Charlie had been the only person who ever called him Logo as a little boy. He was his son in every sense of the word; he was his Logo.

He'd made early arrangements for Logan's education so he'd be prepared to attend the schools that Charles felt were right for him. Throughout those school years, he attended every meeting, game and ceremony at Logan's schools. Still, the proudest day came when Logan accepted his medical degree.

5

Logan's first few years in medical school were very similar to his last two years as an undergraduate. Much of his time was spent either in the classroom or the lab to learn medicine fundamentals, patient care, and prep for his first licensing exams.

It was crucial to pass the exams the first time and move on to the third and fourth years of medical school rather than face the pressure of rewriting.

During his fourth year, he chose rotations in areas that interested him while still taking classes and rotating in hospitals and clinics.

Much of his time was spent on endless tests and essays. He soon learned the value of taking notes, which were essential in learning and remembering when he needed them to fall back on.

It had taken him seven years to complete the steps that would bring him to the point of officially be licensed as a practicing physician. It marked the end of being a student and the beginning of his journey as a doctor. Once he got his internship, he appreciated the many years of long hours and hard work.

His parents attended his graduation. It warmed his heart as Charlie strolled around proudly, snapping pictures of him with his graduating class and accepting his medical degree.

While Logan sat with the others on the stage facing the spectators, he watched his father closely as he wandered about the room for the perfect shot. He was never a big man, but he was of average size and on the slim side. But as his eyes followed him, Logan noticed that Charlie was even thinner now. He made a mental note to ask him about it after the ceremony.

Charlie was the first one at Logan's side once all the grads had received their scroll of papers. Logan towered over Charlie, and he seemed much smaller.
"Are you okay, Dad," he asked, leading him off to one side for privacy.
"I'm not sure, son. I'm waiting on the results from several tests, but don't worry about me. This is your day, and I am so proud of you, Logo!"
Charlie only called him 'Logo' on certain occasions, and Logan thought this must have been one of those times when he felt the need to use it. It was a moment that was always special between them. He still felt uneasy about his father looking so noticeably thin and gaunt.

Logan had settled into his internship at a hospital only a couple of hours from Kanyon Cliffs. He phoned home faithfully asking about his father's health. Isabella always carried a positive attitude and made excuses as to why Charlie wasn't available.
"How is Dad?"
"He seems fine."
"What about the tests he'd mentioned?"
"I don't think it's anything to worry about, Logan. Just come home whenever you have some time, okay?"
"Where is Dad? Let me speak to him."

"Your father is out for a walk, but I'll tell him you were asking after him. Don't worry, Logan, he's okay."

"I'm worried about him, Mom. He was ghastly thin at the graduation."

"He walks all of his weight off, it's a big property, and he loves being outside, you know that."

"Ask him to call me, please, Mom. I mean it." He hadn't seen or heard from his father since his graduation. There didn't seem to be enough time between work and sleep to make a trip home.

He was only four months into his internship when his mother called and asked him to come home. His father had been asking for him.

"I'm sorry, Logan, I thought it would pass, but it has only gotten worse. Please, come home. Charlie needs you."

He thought his mother sounded worried, and now it had his emotions skyrocketing with the worse fears.

When Logan arrived at the castle, Charlie was lying in his bed. Logan appeared in the doorway and gasped at what he saw. His father was just a shell of his former self. Knowing Logan was there, he lifted his hand off the bed and wiggled his fingers for him to come in.

"Dad, why didn't you call me?"

"They told me that I am in advanced stage four pancreatic cancer. What could you do, Logo, that they couldn't, but I'm glad you are here now, my son."

Logan knew by looking at his dad that he was already near death. What he hadn't been aware of was that he had been asking for Logan for several months. But Isabella had been in denial and thought he'd come around eventually.

Logan remembered when his dad had been the household clown for so many years. They jokingly called him the castle-clown of Cliff Haven Castle.

Charles had refused treatment which they said would buy him some time. Still, he felt it was better not to accept it than to allow chemicals to ravage his body anyway. He figured the cancer was doing that all on its own.

Logan sat at his father's bedside every day, and one night while his mother slept beside him, Charlie opened his eyes. Focusing on Logan, he tried to speak. Leaning closer, Logan took his hand as Charlie spoke weakly.

"My son..." he said in a raspy voice, "I am so proud of you, my boy..."

Logan loved this man with all of his heart, and it pained him terribly to have to watch him die. He could do nothing but sit with his father, the person who had been nothing but loving, gentle, kind and generous to him his entire life.

"I'm here, Dad. What can I do for you?" he asked, knowing he was anxious.

"I love you, Logo," he whispered in a voice that was shallow and weak.

"I love you too, Dad," he whispered. Logan tried to keep it together, but when his father called him Logo, it was a special moment between them, and he was about to lose his composure. "Dad," he whispered, "you must save your strength." He wiped at his eyes, but they both knew the end was near.

"I have no strength left to save, my boy. Just remember that I love you, Logo, and never forget your Papa. You… are everything… to me, you and… your mother," he said in gasps. "Wake your Mama… so I can say goodbye… to her, my son, and take… care of… each other for me. My castle… is your castle… now, my boy."

Logan pulled a tissue from the bedside box and blew his nose. Bending forward, he placed a lingering kiss on his father's forehead and then touched his mother's leg. Opening her eyes, he nodded towards his dad, and she knew it was time.

Getting off the bed, she hurried around to his side and grabbed his hand. Logan laid his hand on her shoulder and squeezed. She touched it in acknowledgement.

"I'm here, Charlie, my love," she whispered as emotions built and tears began to run from her eyes unashamedly. She knew that Charlie only had minutes left. He had been her whole life from the time she was barely sixteen. For nearly thirty years, he had been faithfully by her side. She had tried for many of those first few years to give him a child, but every time they had hope, it followed with a miscarriage. Finally, the doctor told them to stop trying and enjoy what they had with Logan before something irreversible happened to Isabella.

"Isabella… my queen…," he whispered with a weak smile.

Logan had seen that look in his father's eye his entire life. He hoped that someday he'd find that kind of love again. His mind when back in time to his last football game. A beautiful young blonde, using the name Slider, had stolen his heart. He hadn't found that connection again with anybody else. Shaking off the thoughts, he looked loving at his parents. In his dad's final moments, he knew that his mother wouldn't want to be anywhere but at his side.

"Be happy, my love... don't be sad... I will love you forever... and beyond. For both of... you... my love for... ever and... beyond..." Charlie lay silent and still.

"Logan?" his mother said, reaching for his hand. Leaning in around her, he pressed his fingers into his father's neck. "He's gone, Mom."

Isabella pressed his hand to her cheek and sobbed while Logan made the necessary calls. Standing behind his mother's chair, he let her spend the last few minutes with him before the ambulance arrived to take him away.

***

Following the service, Logan tried everything in his power to console his mother, but it was to no avail. She needed to cry, she needed to mourn, and she needed to miss him, so Logan stopped trying and left her to grieve. When she was ready, she'd come to him. Logan kept himself busy and mourned his Father in his own way and time but found it was lonely without his mother. He wished they could have grieved together but, Logan was alone too. She ate her meals in her room, and she spent the better part of the day in her bed, crying and missing Charlie. He kept track of her behaviour by questioning her staff since they were the only ones who saw her daily.

Finally, after weeks of seclusion, the day came when Isabella walked down the stairs, fully dressed and ready for the day. She had completed her journey and was about to take on life again. Logan greeted her with open arms and escorted her to the dining room for breakfast.

Isabella returned to her routine by inviting friends to afternoon tea and carrying on with her charities. Finally, after nearly a year, she'd accepted an invitation to a party, but only if Logan would be her escort.

So, dressed in their finest, they headed out to the event. Chatting non-stop along the way, and it was as if nothing had changed between them. Logan was happy that he had his mother back.

As the evening wore on, it looked as if Isabella was the belle of the ball. She was welcomed back into society as if she'd never left. It was plain to see that Charlie's absence had left a gaping hole in their circle of friends.

Isabella carried a glass of wine around with her the entire evening. Taking tiny sips of it now and then, she didn't want to drink enough to cause a waiter to run over and refill her glass.

"It was a great party, Logan," she said on the way home. "Thank you for agreeing to escort me to my first party without Charlie."

"It's nice to see you back to your old self, Mother," he said, smiling at her.

Nearing the castle, Isabella turned slightly in her seat and reached for the dash. "Slow down, Logan," Isabella said, "we're almost home."

Lifting his foot off the accelerator, he pressed down on the brakes.

6

His head felt as if it had been hit with a sledgehammer and was about to explode. As the sedation slowly wore off and he regained his senses, he felt trapped. The cast, the sling, the bandages, the blackness...

Raising his free hand to his head, he moaned with pain, and the doctor hurried to his bedside.

"Logan, I'm Doctor Montgomery. It's about time that you came around. You had me worried."

"How long....?" he started but, his words drifted away.

"It's been a few days, but we've kept a close watch on you. How are you feeling?"

"Like I've been hit by a bloody truck," he said, through the opening at his lips."

"Well, you're close..., not a truck, but a tree," he informed him.

"Oh, God, my mother! How is my mother?" he asked as his memory of their night came flooding back.

"Logan...," he began, and then he stopped, crinkling his eyes in thought, wondering how he was going to say it. "Logan, I'm so sorry.... Your mother didn't make it."

It was as if a bullet had ripped through his chest and into his heart. "Wh... what!?" he cried out into his darkness. Frantically, he tore at the bandages on his head. His doctor had been worried that something like this might happen. He stayed until Logan came around from the sedation. He felt he should be the one to tell him.

"Logan! Logan!" he said, grabbing his hand and pinning it down onto the bed. "You must try and remain calm. I know it will be challenging, but I beg you, please, don't do any more damage to yourself. You must keep your bandages dry, so please settle yourself as much as you can, please! In your condition, you could do more harm than good," he reiterated.

"My condition!? What about my mother?" he yelled as loud as his injuries and bandages would allow. "Tell me everything," he begged.

"I will tell you what I know and what the police have uncovered so far. Make no mistake here; this is in no way your fault. It is still under investigation, but it seems as though you lost control on the curve just before reaching your driveway. It is likely that when you pressed on the brakes, your front tire blew, causing you to lose control of the car, and it veered off into the woods and hit a tree. The rescue team needed the jaws of life to cut you free from the wreckage but, your mother... died on impact. I am so terribly sorry to have to tell you this awful news in your condition, but I felt confident that you'd want the truth, regardless of how bad."

Logan listened, but he was still in shock about the entire nightmare.

"Your leg is fractured in a couple of places, and your elbow took a rather good beating, so it'll be in a sling for a while to help with the bruising," he said.

"What about the bandages on my head? Why am I fully wrapped?"

"Part of a tree uprooted and went through the windshield. It hit your head and pinned you to the headrest on your seat. The impact caused pressure inside your skull; therefore, it is putting pressure on your optic nerve. This kind of pressure can choke the optic nerve and cut off blood circulation. This sort of damage can cause vision loss, severe enough to lead to complete blindness. We won't know anything more until the swelling goes down and we remove the bandages. Do you understand what I am telling you, Logan?"

"Yes, I'm blind, as far as you know," he answered sarcastically, which certainly wasn't his nature, but neither was blindness.

"Well, it's not that cut and dry," he said.

"Then how bloody 'cut and dry' is it then, Doctor?"

"What I'm worried about, at the moment, is your behaviour. There will be no more grabbing at your bandages and definitely no unnecessary movements. If I can't trust you to do as I say, then I will have no other choice than to put you into an induced coma so that your brain and your other injuries have time to heal properly."

Inhaling deeply, Logan tried several times to calm himself down after learning the severity of his condition and that his mother had died. His heart broke at the thought of never seeing her again. To make matters worse, he wasn't even able to mourn her loss. He needed to cry, but he knew he couldn't. He needed to keep his bandages dry, so he had to swallow his pain, close himself off and concentrate on healing. Even so, he really just wanted to go home.

He should have known that it wasn't as simple as just wrapping the wound, let it heal, and all would be well. It's a process that takes time, that doesn't always produce the desired results. So, he had to lay in the darkness, think about his beloved mother, that he will never see again, and wait.

"I'm OK, Doc. Thanks for your honesty," he said, lifting his good hand towards him for a handshake. "How long will I be in here," he asked.

"You're in the ICU for now…."

"What do you mean, 'for now,'" he interrupted.

"For several weeks, you know the protocol for this type of injury. Just imagine what you would do if you were treating an impatient patient of your own," he said as an example.

"Yes, I get your point," he said, a little calmer now. "You'll have my full cooperation, and I'll try to be a better patient, although I can't guarantee anything."

"One more thing, that should relieve your mind, we've done a blood alcohol test on you, and it came back negative. Your mother's test showed a low alcohol level, so there won't be an investigation. It was merely a freak accident, I am sorry to say. I'm sure it happens more than we are aware of, but in your case, no one is at fault." Touching him on the arm, he spoke softly, hoping to rid Logan of any guilt. "I'll check in on you as often as I can, but if you need me, a nurse will page me."

"Thanks, Doc," he said as he heard him walking away.

Dr. Montgomery scribbled instructions on his chart. Instructions were to possibly bring someone in for conversational therapy to help Logan through the trauma of the accident and the grief from the loss of his mother.

Logan lay in the darkness and remembered all the times, as he was growing up, his mother telling stories about her and Charlie. He particularly loved the one about how she had answered an ad and found her Prince Charming. They always brought a smile to her face, and he'd listen like it was the first time hearing them. Sadness crept in at the thought of his mother. Such a beautiful and loving woman..., 'Lady Isabella...,' he thought, 'a proper title for a proper lady.'

7

Logan asked a nurse to contact his butler, Sampson, and instruct him to make arrangements to have his mother cremated and her ashes taken home.

Logan spent several long weeks in the ICU. His head still fully wrapped in bandages, his left leg still in a full cast, suspended on a pulley of sorts, and his arm in a sling from a fractured elbow. Daily, a staff member came in to remove the sling and move his arm this way and that so that it wouldn't seize up.

He'd had lots of time to think and absorb the guilt he'd felt about the accident, and at times he wished that he'd died at the scene too. It would have been better than this. Grief, self-pity and sadness engulfed him to the point where he didn't want to live. His doctor and the nurses were aware and noted that Logan seemed to be slipping into depression, so Dr. Montgomery went ahead with his initial instructions.

***

Alone in his room, weeks after the accident, he heard someone push his door open. Although the head bandage dulled the noise around him, it sharpened his listening skills.

"Who's there?" he asked inquisitively but not interested enough to care.

"Are you Logan Wellington?"

"I am, and who are you?" he said in a demanding demeanor.

"I'm Ms. Slade, and I've been assigned to your case. I want you to know that at any time, if you need someone to talk to, I'm here for you."

"My case!" he said, haughtily towards the muffled voice, "I'm a case now?" Everybody's voice sounded dull and in monotone through the thick bandages. Some days it was difficult to distinguish a male's voice from a female's.

"We are all here to help you, Mr. Wellington, and since you've been through a traumatic experience, I've been scheduled to be here if you need someone. I am only here for that reason, and I will listen."

He didn't even try to correct her from addressing him from Mr. Wellington to Dr. Wellington. 'What would be the point if he couldn't practice medicine again.' Then he remembered that the people they hire get no information on titles for their patients, just their name.

"I don't need someone to talk to," he sneered, "I need to be left alone, and I need to die too!" he said on the verge of tears.

"You can't allow yourself to get upset, Mr. Wellington. Your bandages have to stay dry," she said softly and laid her hand on his arm.

He wanted to shrug it off, but her touch felt warm and comforting.

"Are you from this hospital?" he asked, thinking he might know her.

"No, I work out of a private clinic in Kanyon Ridge," she offered. "Where are you from, Mr. Wellington?" she asked, trying to get him to trust her.

"Please call me Logan and stop with the mister. I am nobody's mister, he said, "and I'm from Kanyon Cliffs, just outside of town.

"Do you mean the cliffs that can be seen from the beach?"

"Yes, it's a nice place, but I doubt I'll ever see it again," he said, turning his head away.

"Were you given that as a definite diagnosis, or is that self-pity I'm hearing?" she asked. "Is there no hope of you ever regaining your eyesight?" she asked while staring at nothing but white gauze bandages with a slit so his lips could move. There were two tiny holes at his nostrils in case he needed oxygen tubes.

"I won't know anything until the bandages come off, but I may as well get used to the blackness. I deserve it," Logan grumbled.

"You do not deserve to be blind," she said, knowing it was inner guilt, "no one does. It was an accident, Mr. Ummm... Logan, accidents happen all the time. Surely, you haven't been living under a bush to know that."

He wanted to smile, but he clamped his teeth together so he wouldn't.

"Sometimes our best is not always good enough. How were you to know the outcome?" Ms. Slade said kindly.

Slapping his hand down hard on the mattress, he said, "I killed my own mother. How can anyone justify that!?" he said in an angry voice. His lips quivered, but he caught himself. Making a fist, he brought it up to his bandaged head, then he spread his fingers out and laid them on the top of his aching head. "Please leave," he asked, "I have a ghastly headache."

Backing away from the bed, her hand slipped off his arm. "Do you mind if I come back?" she asked.

"Suit yourself," he said in a low voice, "I'm not going anywhere."

Turning, she walked to the door, looked back at him and left. He was in a sad and sorry state and probably something that she'd likely add to her notes.

8

After settling down, Logan lay with one arm up behind his head. Like every other night, he became lost in thoughts as he remembered how much he had loved his job as a doctor and how he missed seeing his patients. But there were always thoughts about the accident that he clearly could not forget.

He remembered that days after the accident, while he was still pretty beat up, he'd had a room full of get-well cards from friends and staff, but Preston had to read them to him. He remembered leaving instructions that if any flowers were delivered, send them to another floor or donate them to the local nursing home.

"Give them to someone who could actually 'see' them and enjoy their beauty. Don't waste flowers on me," Logan grumbled.

Preston Kane was his personal valet for as long as he could remember. He was an older Hawaiian gentleman and had joined the staff as a young man. Logan insisted that Preston take a vacation. He didn't care where he went or how long he stayed. "Take my credit card and go somewhere, Preston. I don't require you to come in here every day to sit with me. Don't you think that's a bit much to ask of a valet? You're staring at me while I stare into blackness," he said, using hand gestures back and forth. "You are forced to make conversation, therefore, forcing me to listen. I don't want that. When I'm ready to go home, you'll have plenty of notice, I promise... and Preston, please tell the staff not to visit as well. If I need anything, I will have someone call to have it delivered. I can't expect people to sit here and babysit me. It's absurd."

Thinking about the bandages gave him a smothered feeling for a second. With his head fully bandaged and coverings over his eyes, there wasn't much that he could do except to accept the blackness. 'He deserved to be in the dark," he thought, 'it was where his mother was now.' Morbid visions of his mother trying to climb out of the wreckage haunted him through the day and gave him nightmares at night.

***

Every morning, a team of nurses came by to check up on him and change his bandages and dressings with strict instructions for him not to try and open his eyes.

"I think I get the picture by now. You don't have to tell me every day. I am not a child," Logan reminded them.

"Then stop acting like one," one of the nurses so boldly said.

Chuckling, Logan said, "Well, you got me there. I have been a bit childish at times."

With the bandages removed, they'd shave him carefully while taking particular care around the wounds before applying new ointments and bandages.

"You're a very lucky man, Doctor Wellington," one of the nurses said to him.

"Oh? And how is that?" he asked.

"From the look of your wounds, it could have been a lot worse, damage-wise; I mean," she added, "you should count yourself lucky."

"Please don't call me 'Doctor Wellington' while I'm lying in this bed. Just call me Logan and be done with it. Treat me as you would any other patient and forget about titles," he insisted.

"As you wish," she said and gathered up the tray and left.

Hearing the door click shut, he knew he was alone. He began to go over in his head, for the umpteenth time, the night of the accident.

He and his mother had been looking forward to the house party hosted by one of her dearest friends. Isabella had finally come out of her funk and was excited about the event. She shopped for days for the perfect dress and just the right shoes. She'd asked Logan to escort her since there was no one she'd rather have by her side than her handsome son. They were always as close as a brother and sister since she had been a child having a child, and Logan meant everything to her. At barely forty-six, his beautiful young mother was dead. From the many stories she had told him over the years, he loved and remembered them all. She always said that Charlie had given her a fairytale life. He could hear her voice clearly in his mind, and it was as if she were sitting in a chair talking to him.

9

After six weeks, they cut the cast from Logan's leg and removed the sling from his arm. It gave him more mobility and more time out of his bed. The doctor was pleased with the healing and told him that his leg and arm would be as good as new after several weeks of mild physical therapy. Each day in the workout room, he had therapy on both legs. After all those weeks of bed rest, they needed toning. While there, he asked if he could do more than just leg toning and asked if he could lift weights as well. He was permitted to use only light weights, to begin with, but definitely no straining. Logan looked forward to his time in the gym, but he was only allowed a brief time not to add pressure to his eyes from straining weights. He felt better and less stressed now that he could get out of bed and have someone take him to do a small workout every day. He'd asked for a set of light weights to use in his room and a stretch band to pass some time when he wasn't in the physio room.

***

He'd met with Ms. Slade on more than one occasion. She came, she sat, and she waited. Some days he'd talk, and others, he had nothing to say. Her voice sounded muffled like all the rest. It was difficult to hear through the layers of bandages. She was just another voice that droned on ad nauseam. He'd become exasperated at not being able to see who was in his room or to separate from whom all the voices belonged. He should have known most of them if they were local folks, but no one sounded familiar. If the nurses hadn't identified themselves, then he had no idea who they were either.

When he was confined to his bed and asked to lie still, it was easy to avoid people. Whenever medical staff came into his room to check on him, they didn't know if he was asleep or awake, and at times, he wanted it that way. He'd deliberately not speak so they'd go away quicker. That's how most of his visits with Ms. Slade went also. If he didn't ask who it was, then she didn't disturb him. He was only fooling himself with her because she always touched his arm whenever she entered the room. That was the only familiar thing to him in the days of laying in that hospital bed.

Now that he was more active, she waltzed in and saw the weights and the exercise band. She touched his arm and asked, "Are you awake, or are you faking it, so I'll leave?"

Catching him off guard, he broke into a smile. She saw his lips spread into a grin and said, "Ya, I figured you were faking it. So, what's with the weights? Did they give you permission for limited exercises?"

"Yes, I'm allowed to do some but nothing strenuous," he answered.

"Well, that makes sense. Have you done any today?"

"No, not yet."

"What are you waiting for?"

"Pardon me?"

"You heard me," she said, grabbing the band off his tray table. "Here. Take the end of this and pull."

Taking his hand, she laid the end of the band in his hand, wrapped it around his palm then pressed his fingers closed. Taking the other end, she, too, wrapped it around her palm and braced herself. "Pull!" she instructed.

'What a cheeky creature!' he thought.

"Pull!" she said again, staying braced for, if, or when, he did decide to pull, she'd be ready. "Better still, let's do something else," she suggested. 'This guy is like a mule,' she thought.

"Like what?"

Taking the remote, she pressed the 'up' button and moved his bed to a sitting position. "Swing your legs over the side of the bed," she said in almost an order.

"What the hell are you doing?" he asked, shocked at what he was hearing.

"I'm helping you!" she insisted, "Now swing your legs over the side of the bed," she said and kicked a stool closer for his feet. She had plenty of room of her own, so she braced herself again with one foot behind her and tightening the band for tension. "Pull," she said again.

Lifting the band, he made a tight fist. Watching his hand, she hoped his fist wasn't meant for her personally. Determined, though, she held her stance.

"Are you going to pull or what?" she asked.

He gave a tug and barely stretched the band.

"Well, that's a pussy pull if there ever was one," she teased. She closed her fist around her end and yanked hard, jerking Logan forward. "That's a pull... so come on!"

Pulling harder, he jarred her from her spot, but she held on.

"You can do better than that! You are not going to be a pussy puller, so come on and pull the band!" she insisted.

Pulling again, he brought her forward, surprising her. Backing up, she leaned back and waited. "Bring your arm up into a curl as if you're lifting a weight," she said.

Curling his arm, he pulled his end up into a curl and back again.

"That's better! Go again," she insisted.

Getting into the rhythm, she watched him do ten curls. Then, walking up to him, she opened his fingers, put the band in his other hand, and wrapped it around. "OK, now this one," she said, backing up to get tension.

He curled another ten, and then he switched hands himself. He repeated the sets three times before she stopped him.

"That's enough for now, but let's try something else." She tied the two ends together tightly, then folded it in two. "I'm going to slip this over your feet and around your ankles. OK?" she asked.

"Sure," he said, shrugging his shoulder and thinking that she likely wouldn't leave until she was good and ready. Especially now that she knows he'd been playing possum with her for weeks.

Slipping the band around his ankles, she took his feet and moved them outward. "Do you feel that?" she asked as his calf muscles tightened with each press.

"Yes, I do," he said, and she saw his lips form a smile. "Let me do it," he insisted. Applying pressure, he pressed outwards as his calf muscles expanded. She was counting his reps, and at ten, she stopped him.

"Rest for a few seconds in between every ten presses," she said, "you can't overwork your muscles.

Giving it another try, he rested.

"You're doing fine," she said, resting her hand on his arm.

By instinct, Logan dropped his head to the side where her hand was, and when she noticed his head movement, she pulled her hand away. "I'm leaving now, but if you'd like to add more to your routine, just let me know. I'll be in again."

"When?" he asked, surprising them both.

"Whenever the schedule calls for it, goodbye for now," she said.

"I don't know what your name is?' he said into the darkness, but he was too late. The door had already closed.

After cleaning up, he ate a bit of supper, and while lying in his world of darkness, he thought about his day and Ms. Slade.

10

Finally, the long-awaited day arrived. Opening Logan's door, his doctor's voice rang out.

"Logan, my boy, how about we get those bandages off?"

"Are you serious?" he said, looking towards the voice. "You haven't said a bloody word!" he said, plenty anxious. The heavy bandages over his eyes, face and head had seemed to become his norm after all this time. He hadn't seen the light of day for months on end.

"It's called the element of surprise. This way, you can't overthink the situation."

"Umm...I don't know, Doc... a few days' warning would have been nice."

"Nonsense, let's get this done. There is no time like the present. We've given it lots of time to allow your eyes to heal, so shall we begin? Are you ready?"

He heard a table rolling forward and a basin of instruments being set down. It all sounded familiar since he, himself, had done it many times. He'd wondered recently, 'if the outcome were to be blindness, could he ever practice medicine again?' In his mind, his knowledge was all still there but..., 'probably not.'

"Are you ready, Logan?" he asked again.

"If you think it's time, Doc, then yeah," he said, sucking in his breath and shrugging his shoulders. Rounding out his lips, he exhaled and waited.

"I'm sure you know the procedure, but I have to tell you anyway," he said, pushing a button to raise his bed. "I will cut through the bandage, but you must keep your eyes closed until I give you the OK. Understood?"

"Logan nodded his head as anxiety set in, giving him a rush of adrenalin."

"Do you need a minute?" the doctor asked.

"No, go ahead and get it done," he said.

Logan felt the cool stainless steel from the surgical scissors touch his neck.

"Here we go, my man, step one."

The scissors crunched through the gauze, while each snip brought a bit more relief from pressure that had built up from being tightly wound. Freeing Logan's neck, his instinct to swallow was natural. He heard the scissors as they continued up the side of his head to the top of the bandage, and it was as if a vice had been unclamped, relieving him of the pressure. He felt the nurse slide her hands under his head for support while Dr. Montgomery rolled the remainder of the gauze from his head.

"That is such a relief."

"I suppose it is, and your wounds look good. They are completely healed and with minimal scarring. You might have a few pock-like spots, but nothing that will be noticeable. Being a man helps, too, since shaving keeps our face a bit rough. You might want to get a haircut too. You look like a shaggy dog," he said, laughing and ruffling up his full head of hair. "But seriously, if the scars bother you in any way, then a bit of cosmetic surgery will do the job. Just let me know."

"I'm not worried about that at the moment, Doc, as you might understand," he said nervously.

"I get it. Just keep your eyes closed until after we've had a chance to clean them up. You'll feel a warm liquid now."

The liquid caused him to flinch a bit when it touched his closed lids.

"It's okay; we're just cleaning the medication off your eyelids. There's a bit of crust remaining, and you'll feel a slight pull on your lashes while we soak them to help remove the residue."

"Whatever you need to do." Instinctively, he wanted to open his eyelids. 'Would he ever see again? Would there ever be light in his life again? Was there a possibility that he'd never work again?' His thoughts were conjuring up images and making him uncomfortable. "How much longer, Doc?" he asked.

"We're not quite there yet," he answered, "just a bit longer."

The room was ghostly quiet, and the hum from the motor of a fan or an air conditioner or something was all he heard. Every sound was amplified now with the bandages off so that he became aware of sounds again. Hums, beeps, footsteps and monitors, all sounded heavenly after weeks of muffled and jumbled sounds.

"Are you ready?" asked Dr. Montgomery.

"I think I am, but...."

Try opening your eyes now."

They seemed stuck as he pulled the muscles in his eyelids upwards, but he couldn't feel them lift. "I can't seem to open them, Doc," he said anxiously.

"Calm down," he said, touching his shoulder, "your eyes are open. Just give them a minute. Remember, your eyes and head went through a traumatic time and likely still need time to readjust. Do you see any light at all?"

"Yes, it's a little brighter because I've been in the dark for so long," he answered, "but maybe that's a good thing."

"Do you see any shapes at all?"

No, none," he answered.

"Turn your head to the left, towards the window and tell me if it's lighter," he instructed.

"It seems to be, but I can't tell Doc," he said, "I'm sorry, I'm not of much help."

"You're doing fine," he said, trying to stay positive for Logan's sake.

"I'm not doing fine! I can't bloody see anything! After months of being in those damned bandages, I had hoped for at least a sign that I might see again, but this was totally unexpected," he said on the verge of tears.

"I understand your frustration and disappointment. Truly, I do. We'll try and get you into one of the trials that are coming up...."

Logan raised his hand for him to stop.

"A nurse will give you eyedrops every ten to fifteen minutes for the next hour or so. Then we'll cut it down to several times a day and more medicated ointment, with eye gauze and covers for nighttime. We'll leave you for now but if you need us, just ring your buzzer," he said. Doctor Montgomery set the remote device on the bed and laid his hand on it. Taking his index finger, he moved it across the buttons and explained each one. The up and down positions for the bed, call button and emergency only.

"Thanks, Doc, but I learned the remote a while back," Logan said with sadness in his voice.

"Yes, of course, you did. I'm sorry. Don't give up. Please stay positive, OK?" he asked and called a nurse over to the side to give her instructions for drops.

"Dr. Montgomery?" Logan said.

"Yes, Logan, what is it?"

"When can I go home? I'll have someone there who can do anything that your team has done here. Basically, it's just eye drops from now on anyway, isn't it?" he asked.

"Basically, yes, Logan, all we can do now is use eye drops and wait for further healing. But if you're quite certain you feel you're ready to be released, then I see no reason to keep you here," Dr. Montgomery agreed.

"Surely, with a house full of staff, we should be able to cope with a few bottles of eye drops, thanks Doc. Oh, and one more thing," he said, raising his index finger.

"And what is that, Logan," he asked.

"Could someone please wash my bloody hair?" he asked with a half-hearted grin. He picked it up and pulled his fingers through it, and when he dropped it, it fell onto the back of his neck. He had never had long hair in his entire life.

"We'll get right on that," he laughed.

※※※

Logan asked one of the nurses to call his home and send for Sampson. When he arrived, Logan had a list already made out for him upon his release.

"Please send for Preston at once and let him know they're releasing me soon. Also, I will need someone hired for several days or a week to be at the house while adjusting to the surroundings. Please have someone pack a small bag with some of my clothes to get dressed and get out of these bloody pajamas. I need to feel half human again and buy proper bedroom slippers, the ones with rubber soles... less slipping and all that," he said with a wave. "In the meanwhile, Sampson, have someone clear away obstacles that might be in the way since I'll need a clear walking path inside the house. And I think, for the time being, I'll use the bedroom on the main floor, you know," he said, waving his hand, "the one my mother used years ago, near the old office space."

Sampson was busy writing instructions down while Logan was going over in his head, something he might have overlooked.

"May I make a suggestion, Sir?" asked Sampson.

"Of course. I need all the help and advice that you can give me."

"For the time being, Sir, could I have a few of the staff set up a bedroom for Preston in that old office space? It has a two-piece bathroom attached, and he has a full bathroom upstairs, in his room, for his bath or showers."

"Excellent idea, Sampson. It would be less stressful than being on the main floor totally alone at night. Thank you for thinking about that and if there is anything else that you or the staff can think of, then feel free to work it in."

"Very good, Sir. We'll get right on this list and prepare the house for your return. When shall I pick you up, Sir?" he asked.

"A few days, I suppose, it'll give you time to prepare, and Preston should be back by then. Have you heard from him, by the way?"

"Just a postcard, Sir, and he wrote that he was having a good time. But that was a short while after he'd arrived at his destination."

"Where did he say he was?" Logan asked.

"He didn't say, but the postcard had palm trees on it, so I think somewhere warm, Sir."

"We'll know more when you and I open my credit card statements," he said, laughing. "I gave him carte blanche, so I would expect him to be back in Hawaii having a grand time," he chuckled.

Logan looked forward to going home now that he and Sampson had talked about it and got the ball rolling.

11

Logan was sitting in a leather chair near the window when he heard a knuckle wrap on the inside of his door.

"Who is it?" he asked.

"Just wondering if this is the right room. I'm looking for a passenger."

"Preston, my man! It's so good to hear your voice!" he said, standing up and stretching his arms out to him. Preston gave him a man hug with back slaps and a handshake.

"You look terrific, Sir, and those are pretty cool shades you've got there."

"Thanks, Preston. I'm so happy you're back. How was your trip?"

"It was wonderful, Sir, thank you," he said and leaned in closer to Logan and said, "You know I went to Hawaii, don't you?"

"I didn't know for sure, but I was hoping you had," he said, slapping him on the back again.

"Are you ready?" Preston asked, "the driver is waiting in the car at the entry. In the meanwhile, let me help you into your chair for the ride down."

"Bloody hell," he muttered and found the chair and plunked himself down.

"You know," Preston said, "you sound just like your father at times. You've picked up his words and a bit of his accent over the years."

"Yes, I suppose I have. My father was such a wonderful man, and I still miss him," Logan said softly.

"We all do, Sir, and I agree. He was a lovely man," Preston agreed. "Let's quit fussing about the chair and get on with it; rules are rules, Sir," Preston teased. "And just because you can't see, don't even think that you'll be getting away with anything," he added, trying to lighten the mood a bit.

Logan chuckled, and Preston dropped a bag of supplies onto his lap while he pushed the chair.

"What's all this?" he asked, lifting it into the air.

"It's medications for your eyes, and they gave me instructions that for the next week or so, you'll still need eye patches at night in case you rub your eyes in your sleep. They need to heal more, so you'll need to keep them covered a bit longer," Preston explained. And just to be clear," he added, "we won't be hiring anyone to help out. The staff and I want to do everything we can to make this transition as easy a possible for you."

"Thank you, Preston," Logan said appreciatively.

The driver was waiting by the car's back door when Preston rolled Logan through the automatic doors.

"Mr. Wellington, Sir, it's good to see you."

"I wish I could say the same, Bentley," Logan said, stepping out of the wheelchair.

"I'm sorry, Sir, wrong choice of words," he blushed, but only Preston saw it.

"Relax, Bentley, I'm only teasing you, no harm done," he said reassuringly. "It is what it is for now, and we have to get on with it," Logan added.

The trip home was pleasant enough but strange for Logan to be riding in the dark. Sadly, he missed the beautiful scenery that he'd taken for granted over the many years he'd lived there. The ride seemed short, and before he knew it, they were home.

Stepping out of the car, Preston reached for his elbow, but he refused.

Raising his hand in dismissal, Logan stubbornly said, "I'm OK, Preston, just let me follow you inside," he insisted.

Leading the way, Preston walked at a slower pace while Logan followed with his hand resting on his shoulder. "We're at the front steps," Preston said, "stepping up, Sir, so be careful." Logan felt Preston moving upwards, so when the toe of his shoe hit against the step, he lifted his foot and began his climb. Three steps up and a short walk across the front landing to the door.

Most of the staff were in the front entry when they opened the door. A round of applause exploded, and Logan couldn't help but smile as they all welcomed him home. Raising his hand in acknowledgement, he smiled and thanked them for greeting him. It had been nearly three months since he left for a simple party with his mother, and he has come full circle except without his eyesight or his mother.

"Thank you, everyone. I appreciate the welcoming committee. Thank you all again," Logan said, nodding his head at whoever was there. "Preston, could you take me through to the den and arrange for a cup of hot tea, please? You know the tea at the hospital is ghastly at best. It's like tepid water with a teabag dragged through it."

He heard feet shuffling as the staff went back to their duties. 'Thank God,' he thought, exasperated. 'Whatever does one say to people you can't see?'

Settling in, he waited for someone to come back with his tea. He felt ridiculous sitting in the house with sunglasses on, but he'd feel naked without them now.

Sampson arrived with a tray, "Here we are, Sir, your tea," he said, and as he set the tray down, he noticed that Logan had slipped off his shoes.

"Thank you, Sampson, but one of your helpers could have brought this in."

"I wanted to myself, on your first day home. Sir, may I make a suggestion?" he asked.

"Of course," Logan said, reaching for his tea.

"It might be safer, Sir, if you were to wear your shoes around the house for the time being. Perhaps just until you get your bearing of the house settled in your mind. That way, Sir, if you were to walk into something, then your shoe would take the brunt of it instead of your toes."

Logan pictured his toes bandaged up from being stubbed and smiled. "Sampson, that's a splendid idea and thank you for bringing it to my attention."

"You're welcome, Sir. We have Preston's room prepared in the old office, and he has seen to it that your room has everything you'll need from your upstairs bedroom. Can I get you anything else, Sir?"

"No, Sampson, that'll be all for now and thank you again for the tea. Is the teapot here on the table?" he asked.

"It is, Sir, please be careful. It quite hot."

"I have to start learning a bit of independence, Sampson, and I may as well start with pouring myself a cup of tea. I think I'll be ok," Logan assured him. I have the buzzer if I need anything, and Preston is always close at hand. Thank you, Sampson."

It was strange not being able to see anything and having to feel his way around. Everything breakable was cleared from all the side tables so that his hands wouldn't accidentally knock stuff off. It will take time and a lot of patience for him to get used to living with blindness. He had to move on from thinking about it day and night and occupy his mind in other ways. He was grateful that he had the means from both his father and mother's estate to keep him and the house going, but it didn't ease the disappointment of not being able to work.

As the days wore on, Preston took him riding again, they took long walks with the dogs, and Preston always kept him on the paths and taught him how to use a walking stick for distance and foreign objects that might pop up. He was doing well and learned quickly. He used the stick in the house and soon found his way around the rooms and found it easier to count his steps from here to there. He soon formed patterns in his mind and was able to move about with a bit more freedom. He didn't go far, but at least he didn't have to sit in one spot all day and wait to go to bed at night. He tried to fill his days with activities.

He even tried to learn Braille so that eventually, he might be able to read again. How that would go was anybody's guess. 'Teaching an old dog new tricks and all that,' he thought.

Preston suggested to Logan that he might want to take a walk through the woods and up to the look-off. "Not that you can 'look-off,' Sir, but it's a nice day, and the walk will do us both some good."

"I haven't been up there in years, Preston. That might be fun for us, as long as you're up for it." 'Preston wasn't a young man anymore,' he thought. 'He's been with the staff longer than he could remember. He could have possibly come across with the stones that were used to build the castle a couple of centuries ago,' he thought with a smile. 'Hum... that would make him about two hundred years old, easy.' His thought brought a smile to his face, and Preston asked him what was funny. "You are, my dear boy, you are. Let's go out to the look-off!"

He and Preston walked across the lawn and carefully made their way through the short but stumpy wooded area and out into the open space. They had just stepped out into the field when Preston stopped and turned to Logan and said, "Would you mind waiting here while I hurry back to get my hat and umbrella? It'll be hot out there. I'll only be a few minutes, stay right here, or you can come back with me."

"No, you go on, I'll wait here for you," Logan agreed, "but don't forget I'm here!" he shouted and laughed to himself.

As he waited, he heard the wind picking up a bit, and Preston had had more than enough time to hurry off and be back. Logan had forgotten to bring his stick since

Preston was supposed to be his leader and his eyes. In his mind's eye, he remembered how vast the field was, and he began to saunter across it and into the tall grass. He felt the grass slipping through his fingers as he walked and wondered why no one had mowed.

"Preston!" he yelled but got no answer. "Preston are you there?" he called again. The wind became stronger as he walked farther, so he decided to stop and wait. The wind whipped his hair straight back off his face, but his sunglasses protected his eyes. He felt the wind pull his jacket back as he stood somewhere in an open field. Now he didn't know what to do. He didn't think he'd ever find his way home. And so, he waited.

12

Making her way carefully up the steep and jagged path, she climbed to the top of the cliffs and welcomed the open, flat and expansive field. She'd made the trek many times to be alone and listen to the water crash against the rock cliffs. It gave her a sense of pride, knowing she was the only one who ever dared to climb the steep rocks to this solitary space. Beach walkers wondered what was at the top, but no one ever took the time to do the climb. Today though, as she reached the top, it was blowing nearly gale-force winds, and she was unable to hear anything except the roar. She came out from the sheltered side and into the field. The wind stung as it whipped her hair off her face. Turning away to catch her breath, she caught sight of a man standing on the edge of a cliff. His suit jacket billowing out behind him like a parachute, and his pants legs flapped harshly against his legs while he teetered to keep his balance.

Bending forward, she clasps her hands to her knees to catch her breath from the climb, but she kept her eyes on him. Watching him for a minute from a distance, she couldn't make out who he was. Seeing him on the edge of the cliff set off alarm bells so intense that without a second thought, she struggled to wade through the thick waist-high grass. Making her way towards the stranger, she thought it just didn't seem right that he'd be standing so close to such a high cliff, and she prayed that he wasn't suicidal. She didn't think she'd ever recover if she had to watch someone voluntarily walk off the end of a cliff. The tall grass made it difficult to walk fast, but she kept a good steady pace. He couldn't hear her coming through the roar of the wind.

Rushing up to him, she didn't want to frighten him, and she stopped just a few feet away. His longish, greyish blond hair was blowing straight back from his face as the wind whipped through the emptiness between him and the drop-off, a mere footstep away. He had a couple of days' growths of whiskers, and face-hugging sunglasses hid his eyes. His blank gaze was turned up towards the sun, and the strong winds didn't seem to bother him much, although he teetered from the powerful gusts. A few more steps, and he'd go over the edge. While the winds roared wildly, she wondered if he knew that she was there. Did he even care? Or was he just deeply captivated with the panoramic vista before him? Easing her steps forward, she reached out and touched his arm.

He never flinched since he was used to Preston leading him around. Instead, he cast his eyes downwards, towards his arm, then stared out into nothingness. Wondering, for a second, why that look was familiar, she shrugged it off. It seemed as though he was waiting for someone to appear. The roar of the wind muted the sounds of the raging sea below them.

"Are you OK!" she yelled as the wind caught her breath each time she opened her mouth. Her voice travelled over the current of air, carrying it away. Stepping closer, she moved her hand from the top of his arm and slid it into the bend at his elbow. In response, he pressed against her arm, bringing it closer to his body. Still, he said nothing. Her focus was on this man, and she wondered why he was in an open field and standing on the edge of a sea cliff.

"Don't take another step," she yelled against the wind, and again, her voice was carried off into nothingness. She kept turning her head away from the wind, but no matter where she turned, the wind was there. It whirled and whipped harshly in all directions.

"Why?" he asked in a loud voice but never turned to look at her.

"Why...?" she repeated, "because it's too dangerous, you could fall over."

"Over what?" he asked, staring straight ahead.

"The cliff!" she yelled as the wind cut through her words, "it's only a few steps in front of you." The wind whipped her hair around her face, and reaching up, she dragged it from her eyes and tried, in vain, to tuck it behind her ear. He was much taller than her, and her head barely reached his shoulder.

"Are we at the cliffs?" he questioned.

"Yes! You're nearly at the edge!" she yelled.

"Oh, bloody hell!" he roared as panic and confusion leapt into his throat. Running his hands through his wind-blown hair, he said. "I shouldn't have come this far!" he said, his arms stretched out into the air. "I didn't realize how far I'd walked! Oh, my God!" He became more disoriented and seemed afraid to move one way or the other. She'd heard and read stories about eroding edges of cliffs giving way to weight, and it lay heavily on her mind. Protectively, she raised her hand to his chest, gesturing him to take a step back. She was conjuring up images of him breaking free of her grasp and leaping over the edge. Knowing that if he did, it would take a good fifteen seconds before he'd reach the rocky coast below. 'What thoughts would a person have as the ground came up to meet the body?' she thought briefly before shaking it off.

She felt him move, and she clung to his arm to steady him and to be ready if he made the wrong move. Thankfully, he took a few steps backwards, and she followed. Moving to the back of him, she kept a solid grip on his billowing jacket and coaxed him a little farther ahead. If the wind were to have been behind him, she was sure he'd have sailed over the edge. Slowly, he turned in her direction, causing her to lose her grip on his jacket. His arms stretched out in front of him into the open space, and his hands moved in swim-like strokes as he reached for her. She moved in closer, and his hands grabbed her hair as the wind whipped it in his direction. He touched her shoulder with his free hand. Unsnarling his fingers from her hair, he pressed them behind her head and pulled her into his chest.

"Thank God you were here! Who are you? Where did you come from? Where are we?" he asked. Pinned to his chest, she heard his words clearly as they vibrated into her ear.

Pulling away enough to look up at him, she saw her reflection in his sunglasses, but in his eyes, she also saw pure panic staring back at her.

"What do you mean, where are we? You don't know where you are?"

"I'm afraid I don't but somewhere atop the cliffs. Is that where we are? Could you tell me, please?"

He wasn't looking around or trying to get his bearings; he just seemed to be staring at her. Looking up at him again, she was at a loss for words. She stared across his broad shoulder and down to his shoes. He was quite something to look at, although he could use a shave. He smelled faintly of woodsy cologne, and he looked as if he'd just come from a wedding or a social event. Why else would he be wearing such a snazzy suit with shiny and expensive-looking patent leather shoes?

'Does every living male wear woodsy cologne,' she thought, as it brought back a memory.

"Is there anyone else here?" he asked, still holding onto her.

Looking around, she saw no one. "No, it's just us. Why? Were you with someone?"

"No, well sort of, yes, I was hoping for someone, but that didn't work. Are you sure there's nobody else here?"

"No, there isn't. Can I help you find someone or walk you back to wherever you came from?"

"Would you? That would be splendid!"

'Splendid?' she thought and wondered if there was an accent in there somewhere.

"Show me the way, and I'll get you home, wherever that is," she said, trying to be helpful. Anything involving getting him off this cliff would be a blessing.

"Actually, I don't know where the hell I am. Excuse my language, but I'm afraid I could be lost," he admitted.

Widening her eyes, she moved them back and forth, wondering what to do or say next. 'He must have walked across this enormous field to end up at the edge of this cliff,' she thought, 'so, how could he be lost?'

"OK, we can do this," she said, but likely only the wind heard her words. "Did you walk straight when you ventured out?" she asked, looking into the man's eyes. His sunglasses were darker than usual, but she could still see his eyes. He closed them as if in thought.

"I think I did, yes," he said vaguely, trying to figure it out.

"What do you mean, you think you did?" she asked.

"Well, you see, Preston was taking me for a walk, but he forgot his umbrella, and so he went back for it, but he's not returned."

'Preston? Umbrella? What are you, British?' she wondered. "OK, so who is Preston? And where can we find him?"

"You see, that's where it gets confusing. I don't know where he went, and I only know that he never came back. While I was waiting for him, I just started walking and thought perhaps he'd catch up. Still, the old boy probably forgot what he was doing and, therefore, forgot about me too."

"Old boy?" she asked, stretching her neck forward as if she hadn't heard correctly.

"Preston, he's my personal valet."

'Of course! A personal valet, why didn't I think of that!?' she thought.

"He's been with me for so long," he continued, "I can't remember when he wasn't. He must be somewhere about; surely, he wouldn't just disappear and leave me out here to fend for myself." His voice was steady and pleasant and not a bit annoyed but showed concern for this Preston guy, who seemed to have gone among the missing.

"So obviously, you live around here," she said more to herself than him, but he heard.

"Yes, somewhere, but I'm afraid I don't know where."

'This just keeps getting weirder and weirder,' she thought, opening her eyes wide and nodding her head.

As a child, she'd climbed up here, for some alone time in this field, almost daily but never knew of anything beyond it, and she never ventured farther than the grassy area. It was plenty large enough without looking for more. She wouldn't have thought twice about looking into the woods or searching for other areas; she was content to be in the field. Her climb up was only to listen to the waves crash against the rocks and lay on the grass and watch birds and gulls fly over in search of food or to gaze up into the blue sky looking for shapes in the clouds. But to come up here and find a man on the edge of a cliff was the last thing, or in this instance, person, she expected to find.

"Are you alright?" he asked, bringing her back to the moment.

"Umm, yes, I'm fine, but we have to get you home."

"That would be grand, but how will we do that?" he asked her.

"So, when I saw you first, you were standing over there," she said, turning him back around and pointing to the spot.

She was close enough that he felt her arm go up, so he reached out and touched it and followed it to the end of her finger. Squinting in thought, she looked up at him and saw that his eyes were closed again. 'Ok, so maybe he's getting his bearings,' she thought.

"So, again, when you walked out this far, did you walk straight, or did you wander around in other directions?" she asked.

"Straight, I believe," he said honestly.

"You don't sound sure...," she said uneasily.

"I'm quite sure I just walked straight out," he said, trying to reassure her.

"OK then, let's turn you back around, and we'll head straight back and see where we end up," she said, trying to sound confident. Time was passing, and she had to get him out of this open field. Putting her arm through his again, she felt him squeeze as a sign that he was comfortable with her decision. Walking across the grassy field, she felt the tall grass tickling her legs. The wind had died down considerably since they were farther away from the cliff, so they no longer had to yell to be heard. Looking up at him again, she leaned forward and noticed that he still had his eyes closed. Stopping in her tracks, she stepped in front of him. It was out of her mouth before she even thought about it.

"Why are you walking with your eyes closed, you could be helping me here, but instead, I'm doing all the work. If you want to get home, then I suggest you open your eyes and help me get you there."

A smile passed his lips, and he could envision this feisty lass pointing out the obvious. Reaching up, he slowly pulled the shades from his eyes. "I'm afraid I can't be of much help, you see, I'm blind."

"Blind?" she repeated. Leaning in closer, she peered into the strangers' eyes. What she saw was a gorgeous pair of blue-green eyes that she'd seen only once before, and they reminded her of high school, football and someone named Logo. He was looking straight at her, but he couldn't see her. Like an idiot, she waved her hand in front of him but got no reaction.

"Did you just wave your hand in front of me?" he teased.

"Are you sure your blind?" she asked.

He burst out laughing at her directness.

"Do you mind if I ask you what your name is?" she asked.

"Oh, I'm so sorry, that was rather rude of me. Yes, it's Logan... Logan Wellington," he said, reaching out his hand, "and you are?"

"Logan Wellington! ... *the*... Logan Wellington?" she said in a high-pitched voice and her eyes bugging out of their sockets.

"Well, I'm not sure now," he laughed. "When you say it like that, am I a bad word around here?" he said with another chuckle. "Do we know each other?"

Closing her eyes, she covered her lips with her fingers as if to stuff the words back in. 'Oh my God!' she thought, taking a step away as the pictures began forming in her head. 'Bandages, hospital... oh God, this was *the* Logan

Wellington! Not that there could have ever been two. No wonder he didn't know how to get home! You are such an idiot; you should have realized something was wrong!' she scolded herself for what seemed like minutes before he touched her arm to reassure himself that she was still with him. She hadn't recognized him because she'd never actually seen his face before. 'Oh, dear God! Will he be able to put two and two together? Will he figure out who she is?' she wondered. Forcing herself not to panic, she focused on his words.

"Well?" he asked, waiting for her to answer.

"I'm so sorry," she said in a rush, putting her hands on the sleeves of his jacket. He stiffened slightly at her touch and wondered why it affected him.

"I didn't realize I had said it aloud until after I did. You took me by surprise, that's all," she said, hoping to change the subject. "Logan, I am so sorry. I should have realized something was off when you said you were lost. Please forgive me for being such a dumb ass," she begged.

"Darling girl, how were you to know about my blindness? I should have explained the situation to you, but I got confused once Preston left. I never had to explain anything to him, so I forgot to explain it to you. I am ever so sorry, my dear, so please forgive me for being a dumb-ass too," he said with a chuckle. His good nature made her feel better, and once she knew she was in this alone, it made her think clearer. She slipped her arm through his again; it felt natural, and she wasn't disappointed when she felt the squeeze.

Looking ahead, she saw a stand of trees and finally saw it! A beaten-down path leading into the wooded area.

"I think I may have found where you came out from," she said, releasing his arm. "Stay here, and I'll be right back."

"Where are you going?" he asked into the blackness. "Don't leave me here, please," he said in a pleading voice. He was sure she'd run off and left him alone.

"Miss? Miss? Dammit, I don't know what your name is!" he said with an outstretched hand, but she wasn't there to hear his plea.

Running into the woods, she wanted to see where the path led before bringing him in through the rough ground. She was only a few feet in when she tripped and fell. Falling flat on her stomach, she expelled the air from her lungs. Taking short, stabbing puffs, she wondered if she'd ever breathe right again. It hurt to inhale even with the smallest of pants, but she had to get her lungs inflated again. 'You have to breathe,' she told herself and continued to inhale as long as each breath would allow.

"Miss? Are you there?" he said louder, and this time she heard him.

"I'll be right back," she yelled through the trees, "stay there!"

"That's what Preston said!" he yelled, reaching his hands out into the open space. Dropping them at his sides, he realized that his legs were starting to get tired from standing for such a long time. Bending his knees, Logan sat down on the soft grass and stretched his body out flat on the ground. 'This is a good place to wait for her to come back,' he thought. He let his mind wander back a bit... to Charlie.

'Lord Charles Wellington III,' he thought, 'had proudly given him his last name.' No one, to his knowledge, had ever known that he wasn't Logan's father. They never kept the truth from him, and he didn't care about anyone else being his dad except Charlie. He wasn't given the title of 'Lord' because of the bloodline, but it was always an option if he'd chosen to take it. He was the only father he'd ever known, and because of Charlie's acceptance, he'd led a privileged life and went to the best schools that money could buy. He'd paid Logan's university tuition, and no one was more pleased than his dad when he'd received the title of Dr. Logan Wellington. Logan smiled at the remembrance of his dad.

He'd gone off to Kanyon Crossing, several hours away, to work in a hospital, and made trips home as often as time would allow. He loved the castle, the grounds and the sea cliffs. It was quiet there, and he'd spend time wandering around the acres of property or take drives in one of Charles' cars, mostly his snazzy Rolls Royce or his Bentley. He'd had many to choose from, including his own jeep, and they were his without asking. He'd drive through the countryside or be satisfied to sit at the beach at the edge of town and look up at the cliffs that led to Cliff Haven Castle. One day, as he sat looking towards the cliff, he saw someone climbing up the side. Whoever it was, was only but a speck moving upwards, and he couldn't tell if the person was male or female. He couldn't help but admire the courage it would take to climb that high.

A sadness fell over him as he lay in the grass, alone and waiting.

'If there was any consolation in this,' he thought, 'his father and mother were reunited and in a place where they would always be together.'

"Logan? Logan!?"

Hearing his name, he was sure it was his mother's voice.

"Logan!!!?"

He sat up and got to his feet at the sound of her voice.

13

Pulling herself together, she was finally able to take normal deep breaths so that she could get back to Logan. Coming out into the field, she didn't see him, and it was as if her heart had completely stopped. She couldn't breathe as panic overcame her. Questions flew through her mind in a flurry.

'Did he try to follow her and got turned around?

Where did he go?

Why did she leave him alone?'

Suddenly the beat of her heart picked up speed and was pounding quick and loud.

"Logan!" she began frantically calling his name. "Logan! Where are you?" Scanning the field over quickly, she turned and spun in a circle, hoping to catch a glimpse of him. Clasping her hand against her forehead, she was nearly faint with dread. "Logan...," she whimpered and then in an adrenalin rush, she was way past bellowing and found a high-pitched scream, "Logan!!!?"

✴✴✴

Hearing her voice, he let his memories go and sat straight up, then got to his feet. He was still in the same place as where she'd left him.

"Oh my God, Logan!" she breathed as relief spread across her body. Her feet were tangling in the waist-high grass as she rushed towards him, but she stayed upright. He could hear her footsteps coming towards him, and he put his hands out to her. She went past his hands and into his chest, causing him to wobble for a second from the impact.

Wrapping her arms around his back, she felt him encircle her.

"Thank God! I couldn't see you when I came out of the woods, and I thought you'd wandered off again." Lifting her cheek from his chest, she reached up and put her hands on each side of his face. "You nearly gave me a heart attack," she said softly. His whiskers pricked her thumbs as she stroked them on across his cheeks, and she was greatly relieved knowing he was safe. She couldn't take her eyes off him, and so she just stared. He was gorgeous and gentlemanly. She could tell that he was kind.

At that moment, something changed. She envisioned a football player; he remembered holding a similar tiny cheerleader. Was it an old familiar longing from days gone by or something more recent, or were they both just being ridiculous?

Standing still, he waited for her, and she knew he was waiting. Seizing the moment, she pressed her fingers on the back of his head and drew him down to her. When their lips touched, they inhaled deeply at the sweetness. Memories flowed between them that neither had forgotten over the years. The kiss brought them back… but… back from where?

Bringing his hands up to her face, he drew her in closer and kissed her deeper and with more passion. He had only had these feelings for one other girl. One that he'd never forgotten but couldn't find after their first and only encounter. He was completely overwhelmed with this woman, and he didn't even know her name. Breaking the kiss, so they could both breathe again, he tucked her head into his neck and held her tightly against him. "Oh my God, woman!" he said, breathing into her hair. She closed her eyes, and tears slipped out and onto his shoulder, and she just nodded. 'That kiss, I thought I'd never feel this way, ever again.' He felt the nod against his palm, and then he heard a brief sniffle. Pulling her away from him, he touched the sides of her face and ran his thumbs across her cheeks. "What's the matter, my darling?" he asked softly.

"I don't know, I just feel... so... alive again and relieved, I guess. I was... so... scared when I couldn't see you," she stammered and wrapped her arms around Logan again. Cradling her head with one hand, he wrapped his free arm around her waist.

"When did you eat last? You're very tiny," he joked, trying to brighten her mood. She began to giggle at his humorous attempt to cheer her up. Pushing away from his chest, she put her hands on his arms and gave them a quick shake. "I'm serious; I was really worried."

"I'm right here. I just had a bit of lie down," he said, pointing to the ground. "I couldn't very well stand out here, alone, like a scarecrow. You left me here to die!" he teased, throwing his hands into the air dramatically. But realizing the silence, he reached out for her again to be sure she was still there. Without even the slightest hesitation, he wanted to kiss her again and re-live that feeling. He bent his head towards her, and she took it from there. Raising onto her toes, she pulled him in for another kiss. He moaned as he mashed his lips onto hers, and a quick audible 'umm' escaped from the back of her throat. Offering her his tongue, she accepted it willingly, causing him to groan and pull her even closer than she already was. Feeling his passion growing against her, she was losing her common sense. His kisses were intoxicating, and she wanted more and silently prayed for them not to stop. Pulling his head in for an even deeper kiss, he slid his hands down to her bottom, pulling her closer against his erection. The feel of her body against him was more than he could stand. Her fingers began to tingle, and she couldn't breathe. She felt as if she were hyperventilating.

"Logan," she said, breathing his name. It was as if she'd tossed gasoline into the flames of an already out-of-control blaze. Bending at his knees, he brought her down with him and gently laid her down onto the grass. Pulling her close to him, she tossed her leg over his hip and dug her heel in to draw him closer. He was about to lose his mind, and for the first time, in what seemed like a long time, he wished for his sight back so he could see this lovely creature that he was holding in his arms. Reaching his hand down, he felt her bare leg as it draped over him. Feeling his way up, he realized she was wearing a skirt, and it had worked its way up to her hip. Her skin was as soft and smooth as rose petals as he moved his hand up and down her leg. Rolling slightly off her, he gently ran his hand back up her leg. Curling his middle finger around the top of her panties, he pulled them down. It was like deja vu all over again. She pulled her leg free, and he let go. Running his hands up her tiny body, he tried to envision in his mind just what he was holding. But he let that drop when he felt her unbuckle his belt, twist the button loose and unzip his trousers. Pulling him free from his underwear, she squeezed him, causing him to groan as he kissed her deeper still. He couldn't get enough of her, and he ached to be inside her.

"You're driving me crazy, you know," he whispered against her lips. His words weren't fully off his lips when he felt her rub him against her wetness. Finding the spot, she lunged upwards, and he plunged slowly, and deeply, inside her. He filled her entire body with pleasure. She arched her back and accepted all of what he was offering her. Drawing in a deep breath, they reached a place where neither had been in a long time. It seemed like only seconds, and her body began to tremble. "Logan! Logan! I can't hold it!" she whimpered into his shoulder.

"Let it go, my darling."

Reaching their climax together was like soaring over the edge of the cliff that she'd been trying to save him from falling off.

Breaking the silence, she said, "Logan, what the hell was that?"

"I believe it's called Heaven," he said as he remembered a time he'd been there in the past.

Collapsing beside her, he gathered her up in his arms and pulled her close to him. He wanted to keep her close and never let her go. He already knew that he loved her the second she threw herself into his arms when she thought he'd gone missing. He'd never felt any more at home or at peace than he did right here in the middle of a field. Dropping her leg over his waist again and pulling herself closer, he tucked her into him just like she belonged there. Taking a moment, he absorbed 'feelings,' something he thought he'd never have again.

"What are you thinking about?" she asked softly.

"Truthfully?" he questioned.

"Always," she said, kissing his cheek.

"I'm thinking… that I'd like to know the name of the woman I just made love with," he said. She felt his cheek spread into a grin.

"Bella," she whispered, "Isabella."

"Are you serious?" he said, his face crumbling into a frown. He sat straight up, and suddenly Isabella was frightened that she might have said something wrong.

Sitting up, she turned her body to face him. He had his forearms dangling across his knees, and his head was toward the ground. She put her hands on his arms, and suddenly, he had that feeling again like he's known her from somewhere.

"Yes, Logan, I am serious. My name is Bella. Why? Why did you turn away from me?"

A tear slipped from each of his eyes, and when he reached for her, she straddled him, and he drew her in and held her close. Holding him tightly, she hoped her name hadn't offended him in any way.

"Logan? Are you OK?"

Raising his hands, he gently touched the sides of her face. Closing his eyes, he traced his fingers slowly across her smooth forehead, over the indents of her eyes and moved on to the shape of her nose. Then he spread his fingers across her cheeks and down to her chin and all the way down her neck to her shoulder bones.

"What colour are your eyes?" he asked.

"Green," she answered softly.

"Your hair?" he asked, holding a long strand between his fingers and thumb.

"Honey blonde," she said.

He parted her lips with his thumb and ran it along the front of her teeth. "Nice teeth," he said with a grin.

"What am I, a horse?" she laughed.

"OK," he said, "this is a question that no woman wants to be asked."

"If I said I was seventy-eight, would it make a difference?" she teased before he had a chance to ask the question.

"Hmm," he said thoughtfully, "maybe not today, but if it's true, then you're in great shape for an old gal," he said, teasing her back.

"And you wouldn't be the least bit concerned if you'd just made love to a granny?"

"Oh, good Lord, I'd be appalled!" he snorted and laughed.

"I'm nearly twenty-eight," she answered truthfully, and I weigh one hundred and ten pounds. Anything else?"

"Yes, I have one other," he said, sounding serious.

"What's that then?" she said, bracing herself.

"Who named you Isabella?"

"My father insisted on naming me, and I think it was his grandmother's name from his mother's side. Why?"

"It was my mother's name."

"Shut up!"

"I'm serious. It blew me away when you said it. I lost her just recently," Logan said, with sadness in his voice.

"I'm so sorry," wondering if she should say something.

"Thank you, but don't be. I'm sorry enough for both of us," Logan said sadly.

She put her arms around his neck and laid her head on his shoulder. He ran his hand up and down her back and then turned his face towards her and whispered, "You're quite beautiful."

"You can tell just by touching?"

"Indeed, I can."

"Well then, thank you, I think you are quite handsome too," she said, planting a kiss on his lips.

"Tell me about you now," she said.

"What can I tell you that you can't already see?" he teased.

"I don't know how old you are," she said.

"I've just turned thirty last weekend," he admitted.

"Well then," she said, "happy belated birthday." She would have taken him for a little older, but he was a bit scruffy. His longish blondish hair that she had mistaken earlier for greying was actually sun-streaked. He had a boyish grin that showed a beautiful set of teeth and full kissable lips that she adored. He was easily six foot two, which is why she needed her tippy toes to kiss him. She knew already that she loved him, and they only met just a few short hours ago. Having no idea where this would go, she knew in her heart that she'd cherish this day her whole life long.

"Do you think we should get you home now? Is anyone looking for you?" she asked as she got up off his lap and stood up.

"I'm going to say no, or they'd be here by now," he joked as he lifted himself to stand up too. He shuffled his twisted trousers around so he could zip, button and buckle himself back together. At the same time, she stepped into the other leg of her panties and pulled them up. Neither of them had an embarrassing thought about what had happened. It was as if it was a normal thing for them to be doing.

"Bella?" he said.

'Here it comes,' she thought, 'he's going to tell me that they'd made a big mistake.'

"I hope you're OK with what happened here today. I know it was a bit unusual for both of us, I suppose, but please don't allow it to end here."

Throwing herself into his arms, she held him tightly. "No, Logan, I don't want it to end here either."

Walking arm and arm, they headed off into the trees. Pulling Bella close, he whispered, "This has been quite a day."

Suddenly Bella let out a scream as they came upon where she had tripped earlier. "Oh, my God! Logan! It's a man lying there! I must have tripped on his foot when I came through here the first time. I went flat on my face and knocked the wind out of me. I didn't notice him," she said in a rush.

"Take me to him," he demanded.

"He's right there," she pointed stupidly. "Bend over. Touch him."

With both hands out, Logan felt around on the man. First on his chest, then he fumbled for his wrist to feel for a pulse. "His pulse is vague, but he has one," he said and then moved him to one side and felt behind him.

Passing her a wallet and a flip phone, he barked, "Call 9-1-1."

"I don't know where we are! How can I give them directions?"

"What is in the wallet?" he asked.

Flipping it open, she found a driver's license. "Oh my God, Logan, it's Preston!"

Her hands shaking, she dialed 9-1-1.

"9-1-1. What is your emergency?"

Giving him the brief details, she told him the man was still breathing but that Logan was calling it a heart attack. Giving him the address from Preston's driver's license, she pleaded with the operator to hurry.

"Stay on the line so that we can maintain contact. Is someone doing CPR?" Bella turned around, and Logan was pumping his chest like a pro.

"Yes, he is," she answered.

"Come on, Preston, don't you die on me now!" Logan demanded.

"Tell him not to stop compressions until the paramedics arrive."

"I will, and please hurry!" she said frantically.

"The ambulance is on its way, Logan," she said.

"Thank you," he said, still pumping Preston's chest. "I need you to go through the trees and out into the yard and wait for the ambulance and bring them back here. Can you do that?"

Noting that he didn't need instructions for CPR, she let that drop. "Is it far?" she asked.

"No, just passed the trees, you'll be fine, just go," he begged.

Turning on her heels, she fled through the trees and followed the path until she broke through into a clearing. Stopping short, she couldn't believe her eyes. Sitting before her was a grand castle, like something out of a fairytale. It was spread across a beautifully manicured property with a tree-lined driveway. A garage that stood behind the castle was almost as large as the castle itself. It looked as if it would hold at least a dozen vehicles. The screaming siren brought her back to focus on Logan and Preston. The ambulance raced up the driveway, leaving a trail of dust in its wake. She ran closer, waving her arms to show them where she was. Tearing across the lawn, they stopped at the tree line.

"Hey, guys! He's just in there!" she yelled as the siren died out.

Grabbing a board and medical kits from the back, they raced with her through the trees until they found the two men. Logan was sitting on the ground with Preston propped up against his shoulder.

"Doctor Wellington. It's Simon and Zack. It looks as if you've still got the touch!" they laughed and went to work on Preston, checking his vitals and listening to his heart. Logan got to his feet and moved carefully away.

"He's got a fairly strong heartbeat, Doc. Good job, my man!"

Logan just smiled and shook his head. "Bella?" Logan asked, reaching out for her. Slipping her hand in his, he squeezed it and thanked her for guiding the EMT's back.

'Doctor Wellington? There is a story here!' she thought.

As if reading her mind, he said, "Yes, I have some explaining to do."

"Well, yes and no," she said.

"What do you mean?"

"You only have to tell me if you want to. Your life is none of my business." She certainly didn't want him thinking of her as just being nosy, and besides, she had her own secrets.

"How about if I want to make it your business," he said, leaning and whispering in her ear.

"Then that's your business," squeezing hands at the same time. They watched the men strap Preston onto the board so they could carry him out.

"Again, great job, Doc. You've likely saved his life," said Simon. He touched Logan's shoulder to let him know he was close. Logan reached out to shake his hand.

"I know it's none of my business, but I hope you will reconsider coming in for the experimental testing that is available. You know we always need guinea pigs," he said, slapping Logan on the back. "Besides, more than enough time has passed, so get off your ass and make the call. Always nice to see you, pal. You too, Bella."

Logan caught Simon's words to Bella but put them aside, thinking that she'd introduced herself earlier.

"Thanks, Simon. I appreciate your concern."

"Any time. You know we need you at the hospital."

Taking a step forward, Logan followed Bella through the woods and out into the clearing.

"And I suppose this shack belongs to you?" she asked.

He laughed, dropped her hand and put his arm around her shoulder, pulling her closer.

"You suppose correctly, my dear," he joked, "Welcome to my humble cabin." Laughing, they crossed the lawn. He was familiar enough now that he could guide Bella to the front door. Pushing it open, they faced an entry nearly full of staff members. All eyes were on Logan.

"We are sorry to intrude, but we were wondering about the ambulance. We were worried about you, Sir."

"Sampson, I'm fine, but poor old Preston has had a heart attack while up in the woods as we were taking a walk. Ms. ... um... Bella was a great help and has brought me home."

Nodding slightly in her direction, Sampson turned back to Logan. "We are sorry about Preston, Sir, but shouldn't you get some rest yourself?"

"I will, Sampson. First, though, I think Ms. Bella and I deserve a decent meal, don't you?"

"I do indeed, Sir. We'll go and set up the dining room."

"Sampson, could you please set up a small table in the den next to the fire instead of the large dining room?"

"As you wish, Sir," said Sampson, bowing slightly towards Bella before leaving the room.

"He's a bit of a snob, but don't mind him. He has been with the house for a hundred years. He was here when I was born, but he still loves what he is doing. Let's go into the den, Bella," he said, reaching for her hand.

He knew his way around the house quite well and led her directly into the den. It was cozy and elaborate, but so was the entire place. She couldn't help but gawk around the entrance while Logan was chatting with Sampson. She was totally in awe. As huge as it was, one would think it would've been just as cold and creepy as it looked from the outside, but it was lovely, warm and surprisingly comfortable.

Sampson arrived with a much younger man who carried a huge tray and sat it on a buffet hutch. In what seemed like lightning speed, they had a table pulled up in front of the fireplace. A tablecloth that was draped over his arm was shaken out and flung neatly over the table. Bringing their tray closer, he sat it on a side table and began to set their place setting in front of them. Cutlery, glasses and napkins set to perfection even for a small luncheon.

"Thank you, Sampson... and your... um, helper...," Logan said, not sure who was with Sampson.

"Ben, Sir," Sampson added.

"Thank you both, but we can take it from here and serve ourselves," Logan insisted.

"Will there be anything else, Sir?"

"Yes, Sampson, please send someone to the hospital to check up on Preston. Ask them to keep him company if he wants any, and later on, I'll need the car brought around to drive Ms. Bella home. I'll ring when we are ready. Thank you, Sampson."

Bella sat straight-backed in her chair, not knowing what else to do in these elaborate surroundings. 'How does one act in a place like this,' she wondered.

"Are you OK, Bella?" Logan asked, reaching across the table for her hand.

"I am. I'm a little nervous, to be honest," she admitted.

"Pfft!" he said, flipping his wrist at her, "don't be, make yourself at home, I insist, and if anyone looks at you sideways, you let me know," he joked. "You can consider this just a simple house with way too many rooms. So how about we take our plates to the buffet and you can fill mine for me. I'm sure there's nothing on there that I don't like..." he said, giving her a nudge to indicate he was joking. "They wouldn't dare!" he said with a belly laugh. She loved his sense of humour.

"You know they are all intimidated by me," he said. "Me!" he said in a pitched voice, "A blind man! They could all be doing monkey shines behind my back, and I wouldn't even know it," he laughed. But he knew from all the years living there that he had dedicated and loyal staff.

After a pleasant meal and conversation, Bella thought that Logan should get some rest, so she insisted on going home.

"It has been a long day for you, Logan," she said, "starting with a brief walk and to a full day of...,"

"Of what?" he interrupted with a devilish grin. "Passion? Excitement? Daring to be daring? Critical situations? That used to spell fun back in the day. It has been much too long since I've had any fun," he said. Leaning sideways, he pushed a button to summons Sampson.

"So, thank you, Bella, for showing up today, or they might be scraping my lifeless body off the rocks below the cliffs. That is if anyone were to have witnessed my fall. It was obvious that poor Preston wouldn't have come back for me either. What a ghastly thought, being out in the field and only a few feet from death and no one to come to my rescue..., except you. Bella, my heroine," he said, spreading his arms dramatically.

"What a horrid thought!" she said, "but, seriously, Logan, you were, literally, just about two steps away from walking over the edge today."

"So, does 'daring' fit into this day at all?" he joked.

Slapping him tenderly on the arm, she said, 'It's nothing to joke about, Logan. You could have died today!"

"Well, at some point, I did mention Heaven," he teased.

"Yes, you did, and it was," she said softly. Raising on her toes, she kissed Logan and said, "Goodnight."

"Good Night, Bella."

Sampson showed her through the entry to the door and then opened the car door for her.

"Bentley will take you wherever you want to go, Ms. Bella."

"Thank you, Sampson," she said nicely, and he closed the door.

'Hmm...' he thought, squinting his eyes. He didn't want her to be nice to him because he didn't want to like this woman. He not only didn't like it that she had the same name as his first Lady Isabella, but she could very well spell heartbreak for young Logan.

14

Bella settled back against the seat and watched the beauty of the winding driveway. It was nicely landscaped and seemed miles off the main route. Bentley watched her in the rearview mirror, and once he turned onto the roadway, he asked for an address. Looking at him strangely, she recited a familiar address and gave him a few directions, and he seemed satisfied.

Dropping her off, he watched her from across the street. She went into an unsecured building and disappeared. He pulled over into the nearest parking spot, hoping to clear up his suspicions. Logan was insistent that he make sure that she got home safely, but, somehow, the place just didn't sit well with him. 'She didn't seem the type, somehow, to be living at an address like this one. Not that it was seedy or anything but just not right for Bella,' he thought. He'd hardly had time to roll his window down when she reappeared. She quickly scanned up and down the street and fled in the same direction from where they'd just come. Hailing a cab, she jumped in, and it hightailed it down the road. Before Bentley had a chance to get the car turned around, they were out of sight, and he'd lost them.

Bella had an ongoing account with the cab company. Having no car, she took a cab nearly everywhere she went and paid off her account at the end of every week. Pulling up in front of her building, they bid each other a good night, and she buzzed her apartment. Opening the door, Bella called out, "I'm home!"

"Hey, Ms. Bella, you were longer than originally planned," Mrs. Perez said, pointing out the obvious with her thick Spanish accent.

"I know, Mrs. Perez, things went kind of crazy on my climb today, but I will pay you extra for your time and trouble."

"It's no trouble, Ms. Bella. Your son is a dream child," she said with a smile.

Pressing some money into her palm, she said, "Thank you, where is he?"

"In his room, reading a book. With all the technology in there and he is reading a book, he is such a good boy," said Mrs. Perez, nodding her head towards his bedroom.

"See you in the morning," Bella said on the way to the door. "And by the way, I stopped at your apartment tonight for just a minute," she said as she lifted her thumb and first finger into an inch high measure and gave her a wink. Mrs. Perez nodded her approval and said goodnight. She was one of the very few people who knew Bella's entire story, and she had given her permission to use her apartment whenever necessary. Tonight was one of those necessary nights.

"Hey, Logo," Bella said, going into his room.

"Hey, Mom, where were you today?"

Shrugging, she said, "On my usual climb, with a few complications."

"You could have called, Mom."

"I didn't take my phone or my keys. It's the last time I'll do that! That's a promise."

Wrinkling his eyebrows, "Mom! That's not cool! What if something had happened and you had no identification?"

"As I said, it was complicated, but I'll do better," she reassured him. "Would you like to watch a movie with me later?"

"No thanks, Mom, not tonight. I want to finish reading this book before bed."

"I'll say goodnight then," leaning in to kiss the top of his head.

"Goodnight, Mom," he said, flipping a page.

Bella took a long, hot and much-needed shower. 'What a day!' she thought as she dried herself off and blew her hair partially dry. Getting into bed, she propped her pillows up behind her and leaned back against them. She thought about her day with Logan, and just remembering how he'd felt in her arms and how he'd made her feel caused her tummy to flip with excitement. Something she hasn't felt in such a long time. 'A long time,' she thought and squinted her eyes, and if time travel were possible, she found herself back to a time and a place when that excitement first occurred. It hurt so much to go back there, but something was niggling at her, and she had to find out what it was.

***

Bella remembered a football game at another school. It was going to be the biggest event of the year. Their cheerleading coach had gathered them together and gave them the news and a pep talk.

"This is going to be the biggest splash of all times for both schools. The good news is, they want you girls there at halftime to entertain! A cheerleading invitation to another school is something that has never happened before in our areas. No high school has ever invited another cheerleading squad to their games. They have always and forever just used their own school cheerleaders. So, this is an honour, girls, and I want you all to do us and yourselves proud!" she said with excitement.

The girls jumped up and down and shook their pompoms high and proud. It was an honour to be called in to cheer for another school.

At the game, no one knew who any of the team players were. They had painted their faces in their school colours of navy blue and red, and they all looked the same except some were taller than others. The girls thought it would be fun, for this one night, to use different last names for each other. They decided that Bella's name would be 'Slider.'

At seventeen and looking forward to graduation soon, Bella was thrilled to be cheerleading at this final game. They went out at halftime and did their routine for a packed stadium that encouraged them by cheering them on.

At the end of the game, with the entire football team gathered around the cheerleaders, they announced that Kanyon Ridge High had outdone themselves. The school was proud to have had them join their school for the last game of the year. Cheers, roars and confetti erupted on the field. Bella had met some of the team members that day, and she was surprised when one of the players walked up to her.

"There's someone who wants to meet you," said a tall and lanky fellow.

"Who?" she asked.

"Go, Slider!" her friends yelled out at her.

"He's right over here," he said, leading her to a group of players."

"Logo! Meet Slider," he said and walked away.

All she'd seen, behind the paint, was a set of blue-green eyes and a wide beautiful grin. Standing next to her, with a huge number sixteen on his jersey, he was several heads taller than she was, and it seemed he'd had a bit of celebratory drink. She wished that she could have seen what he looked like under the elaborate striped paint, but he seemed kind enough. After some chit-chat about nothing in particular, he took her by the arm. Leading her around to the back, they sat on the grass just out of sight of the others. Pulling her close, she was nervous about this overpowering charmer. Even though he had just finished a game of football, he had a woodsy scent that was as intoxicating as his charming self was. Her heart was all a flutter even though she couldn't see his face. Leaning in, he touched his lips to hers and then pulled away. "I'm sorry, Slider, I should have asked your permission," he said apologetically. She sensed that perhaps the drink was wearing off and waned his bravery. Suddenly he became bashful and more of a gentleman. 'You're very pretty, by the way, and I apologize for my behaviour. It seems the end-of-season game night can sometimes get out of hand for us, and we act as if bloody hell has been let out for recess.

"End of the year games are meant to be fun," she said.

"Well, I must admit, I like this one," he said, leaning in to bump her shoulder. Looking into her green eyes, he saw something different in this girl.

"What?" she said, caught up in his stare.

"May I kiss you properly?" he asked.

Nodding her permission, he leaned in, slid his hands under her blonde hair and pressed his lips against hers. Ending the kiss, he reached for her and drew her over to straddle his lap. Her hands touched his arms, and she felt him stiffen a bit. Reaching up, she put her hands behind his head, spread her fingers and pulled his lips to hers. Sucking in his breath, he pressed closer and kissed her harder and hungrier than he'd ever felt before.

"My God, girl, where did you learn to kiss like that," he asked between kisses.

"You're my first real kiss," she admitted against his lips, not wanting to let go."

"I need to get out of this bloody gear," he breathed between pants and kisses.

"I'll help you," she said, yanking the jersey over his head so he could get the shoulder pads off. "Put your jersey back on. It's rather chilly," she said and helped him pull it back over his head. He smiled at her, and she knew she would never forget the look that she saw under all that paint.

Kicking off his cleats, he stepped out of his pants to remove the knee pads and his jockstrap. "You're a bit overdressed," he said with a smile. Bending her head back, she looked up at him. She was wearing her school jacket over her short cheerleading skirt with matching underwear and a sleeveless tee-shirt.

"It's a little cold to be out here naked," she said shyly.

"Absolutely," he said, pulling his jersey back off. "Here, lay down on this and stay covered up," he said, helping her to the ground. Lying beside her, he pulled her into his warmth. Leaning over her, he pressed his lips to hers again, and they were back in the moment. Reaching his long arm out, he made slow strokes up and down her legs. Tucking his fingers around her panties, she lifted enough for him to slide them down. He didn't seem exactly experienced, but neither was she, but they both knew and accepted that they wanted this more than anything.

He fumbled to get where he needed to be, and when he finally hit home, it was almost more than he could bear. If this wasn't Heaven, then he didn't know what was. Underneath him was this tiny frame of a girl who was driving him mad with sweet kisses that were sending him over the edge. She began to tremble and cried out, "Logo! Oh my God, Logo! Something is happening, and I can't stop it. She panted and moved rhythmically with him.

"Let it go, Slider, I'm with you!" he panted. Suddenly, it was as if the earth had opened up and swallowed them whole as they tumbled down into an endless pit of pleasure. Logo was holding himself up so as not to put his entire weight onto her. He was losing his grip and slid to the side but gathered her up and took her with him. He never wanted this day to end, and he certainly didn't want this to be the end with Slider.

"That was a first," she admitted, "and I'm guessing that was an orgasm."

Holding her close to him, he felt this to be the closest thing to love that he'd ever experienced. They had both relaxed enough that they wanted to drift off to sleep when they heard voices. Somebody in the distance had called out that the bus was leaving in ten minutes and for everyone to get the lead out! Now!

Bella jumped to her feet, straightened her clothes out and stepped back into her underwear. Bending her head forward, she quickly ran her fingers through her long blonde hair. Flipping it back up, she tried to fluff it up a bit. She was the most beautiful creature he had ever seen as he watched her tidy herself up.

"Slider, tonight was special for me," he said.

"For me too, Logo," she said, widening her eyes, "if you know what I mean."

"Was I your first?" he asked bravely.

"Yes, you were my first, and I don't regret it. I loved it," Slider said without hesitation.

Getting to his feet, he took her in his arms and held her close. "So, did I, Slider, so did I. Here," he said, picking up his navy and red football jersey, "I want you to have this."

"Really?" she squealed, "your last game jersey?"

"My last high school game. I'm off to university soon. So, take it and keep it, along with my heart."

"Logo, that's so sweet! Thank you!" she said, stretching on her tiptoes to kiss him. A thought came to her, and she dug around in her jacket pocket and brought out a small chain. At the end of it, a small cube dangled from it, a die. Each side had some black dots ranging from one to six, while the side that should have had five dots on it remained blank.

"I know it's lame, but when you add up the pips on all sides, there are sixteen, the same as the number on your jersey. How weird is that?" she asked.

"Very weird, but I like weird," he said, smiling.

"Me too," she said, smiling back. She folded the jersey up and laid it over her arm. The sound of footsteps was closer, and Bella stepped out from under the bleachers.

"There you are!" someone said, "we have to hurry; the bus is warming up."

"I just slipped behind here to pee," she said before someone actually took the time to look in. She didn't take a chance on looking back; she just ran off with her classmates as if nothing extraordinary had just happened.

"Whatcha got there?" someone asked.

"A jersey. I found it on one of the benches."

"Logo smiled and gathered up the rest of his stuff.

Walking back to the bus, Slider couldn't forget that Logo mentioned university. 'So, this is going nowhere,' she thought.

✽✽✽

Coming back to the present, Bella remembered the single night when she'd met Logo. It has always been forever etched into her memory. Being shrouded in mystery from the very beginning only added to the excitement and the thrill of the unknown.

Still wide awake, she slid farther down under the covers and stumbled back to the place where something had ended and something new began.

***

Sitting with her classmates at their high school graduation, she waited for her name to be called to go up and accept her diploma. Her cap and gown felt heavy and cumbersome, and she could feel the heat building up under her clothing. She stretched the neck of her gown to let some heat out or let air in; she wasn't sure which, and she fanned herself with the program booklet. The classmate sitting next to her leaned over and asked if she was ok. She responded that she felt a bit over-heated with the gown on. Finally, they called her name, and as she made her way to the stage, she felt faint for just a second or two. It passed quickly, but she was shaken by it just the same. Once everyone was outside and gathered in groups, they tossed their caps in the air for good luck and adios high school.

***

The weeks passed, and summer was abysmally hot, causing Bella to spend most of her time inside near a fan. There was no place that she could go that made her feel comfortable. She was irritable and upset at every turn.

She'd gone into the bathroom for a cool shower, hoping it would help with the heat. While rooting under the sink for some shampoo, she noticed an unopened box of tampons. She yanked her hand out quickly as if she'd touched something hot. Goosebumps crawled up into her scalp, and a realization caused her to lose her balance. Tipping backwards from her squatting position, she toppled over onto the floor. Staring under the cabinet at the unused box, she wondered, 'When had she had a period last?' Then the horror set in. 'Not since before the football game! Oh my God,' she thought and clamped her hand over her mouth to stop herself from crying out. She knew exactly when because she remembered finishing up her period just before the game, and she'd been relieved.

A knock came at the door. "Isabella? Are you ok?... Isabella?" her mother asked anxiously.

Sitting against the bathtub, in shock, no words would come out of her mouth as tears slid down her cheeks. Her mother turned the knob and opened the door. Seeing Isabella on the floor, she ran to her.

"Bella, sweetheart, what is the matter? What happened? Why are you crying?" Leaning against her mother, Bella openly sobbed. Her mother held her through the worst of it but then insisted that she talk to her.

"What can I do, Bella? Tell me what's wrong," she pleaded.

"Mom, I don't know what to say," she sobbed.

"Just tell me, Bella!" she insisted.

"I think I might be pregnant, Mom," she said and cried even harder.

"Pregnant? Are you sure?" she asked.

"It only happened once, but I haven't had my period since. What am I going to do?" Bella said, reaching for the roll of toilet paper to blow her nose.

"Bella, we'll get you checked out and find out for sure. Get up off the floor and come and talk to me," her mother coaxed.

Dragging in broken breaths, she got to her feet and followed her mother to the living room.

"Tell me, Bella, who is this boy?" she asked.

Hanging her head, Bella pressed her lips together and then touched her fingertips to them. "Mom, it is so hard for me to tell you this, but I don't know what his name is," she sniffled.

"Bella! How can you say that! I hope you're not saying that to protect him! Because if you are, I will find out!" she said loudly. She wasn't angry, but when she got excited, her voice got loud.

"I'm telling the truth, Mom. I truly don't know his name. I met him at the last football game, but we both used a different name. I don't know who he is, I'm sorry, I know that sounds bad, but it's the truth."

15

While holding her tiny son in her arms, Bella knew that she never wanted to forget her baby's father. The only name she knew him by was Logo. She also knew her mother would question the name, but she didn't care. She was going to name her child after his father even though it wasn't his real name. It was the only name she had, so it was real to her. Now that she had a son, she had someone to pass his jersey on to. The jersey had stayed hidden in the back of her closet for months. Now and then, she'd pull it out and bury her face in it and smell the woodsy cologne that still lingered on it. She always wondered why the jersey had only a number when all other games that she was a cheerleader at, the player's names were on the back. It boggled her mind every time she brought it out of its hiding place. It would have eased her mind a bit to have a last name attached to the jersey. It had always remained a mystery.

***

She was fortunate enough to have her mother at home to help with Logo to continue her education. She'd enrolled in an online master's program shortly after learning of her pregnancy to help pass the time. It would take up to twenty-eight months to complete. As the days grew closer to final exams, Bella began making plans of her own. Soon, she would have her freedom and independence, so she began searching the real estate section for an apartment. It had been long and grueling two-plus years, but when her diploma arrived in the mail, it was the happiest day of her life.

Packing up her bedroom and her toddler son, Bella moved to a new apartment and started a new job as a counsellor and a new life. She was fortunate enough to snag a great sitter for Logo, and Mrs. Perez loved Bella's son as if he were her own.

Checking the clock on her nightstand, her trip down memory lane had her wide awake. She hadn't ventured down this path for a long time but today sparked something that wouldn't go away. 'Surely Logo and Logan Wellington couldn't be the same person.' She never really saw his real face that night from so long ago and hadn't at the hospital either, but those eyes and the kisses and the lovemaking. 'Surely, it must all be coincidental.' She'd fallen in love with Logo at a football game, crushed hard on a patient without even seeing his face, and fell in love with Logan today on the cliffs. 'Three separate encounters of blind love,' she thought, 'but surely they aren't the same person! What now?' One thing was for sure; she could never see Logan again. If she had this figured out, then surely Logan would put two and two together and come up with three the same way that she had. Oh yes, she must keep her distance. There was no way she could ever be around him again and not slip up. Her mind was made up. She would never climb up the cliff again.

16

In Preston's absence, Sampson prepared Logan for bed. Helping him in and out of the shower, he laid out his pajamas and robe. Helping him get dressed, Sampson turned down his bed and said goodnight.

'Bella,' he thought. She made his heart beat a little faster at the thought of her name. 'Dammit!' he thought, 'I still don't know her last name. Bloody hell, I haven't got a phone number either!' "Logan Wellington," he said aloud, "you are slipping fast! Where has your mind gone?"

Going into deep thoughts and no one to joke around with, Logan realized now that he'd be eternally grateful to Bella for being on the cliff today. Right time, right place, as they say. Things could have ended very badly for him, and his heart began to pump adrenalin at the thoughts of being mere steps away from death. He never spent a lot of time on the cliffs as a boy, but when he did, it was only to walk to the edge, look out over the view for a few minutes, then leave. He had other stuff to do, like football, soccer and biking.

Going up there with Preston was just for a short outing, and he hadn't realized how far across the field he'd walked, and it hit him again how fortunate he was that Bella was there. 'Bella,' he thought, and he felt his entire being go to mush at the mere thought of her name. Her touch felt familiar, but he could not make a connection in his mind.

Something took him back in time when he'd had finished up high school.

Logan remembered the last football game of the year, and the school had asked him to play. He had been out of school for a year and home on a break from travelling when the coach approached him and asked if he'd join the game for old time's sake.

"There isn't time to put your name on a jersey," he'd said, "but we still have your old number sixteen."

He was glad that he'd accepted after meeting a gal who'd blown him away. 'That cheerleader, Slider, from another high school,' he thought, 'she was such a beauty.' That long blonde hair and those alluring green eyes had made his heart pound, and they seemed to look deep into his soul. He knew he'd never forget her; she was his first and only true love. He thought about her for months, even years after that night. He remembered her walking away from the bleachers to protect him. Watching her walk away was the hardest thing he'd ever done, but after she'd told her friends that she was there alone, how could he run after her still half-naked?

He remembered kicking himself for days for not being honest with her. 'Logo,' he thought, 'only one other person had called him that, and he didn't know why he'd used it that night. Surely, she must have known it was fake, but then again, who calls themselves Slider?'

Settling in with his thoughts again, he remembered trying to find her. But he had no luck in finding out who she was. It wasn't for lack of trying either. He'd even driven to her school, but no one had heard of anyone named Slider. He never came right out and said that he was looking for a girl because even he had trouble believing it was a girl's name. Graduation was just around the corner, and if he didn't find her before then, he knew he'd be out of luck. He'd spent several afternoons parked out in front of the school until a police officer pulled up and told him to take a hike. Defeated, he headed home, no farther ahead than when he'd started. 'Damn! I'm screwed.' All he had now were memories of how she'd made him feel, how much she seemed to care for him and a die that he still had on his key ring. He loved that she'd admitted that he'd been her first. It was the one thing that would always be indelibly imprinted in his memory.

This day would always be memorable, too, after meeting Bella. He'd never completely forget about Slider, but this was today, and he'd found Bella and a future. Slider was in his past. His mind went through what he could remember without really seeing anything. 'Making love to Bella,' he thought, 'how could any man forget that. Making love to someone without knowing their name is almost unheard of,' he chuckled to himself. But then again, that's precisely what had happened with him and Slider, fake names, true feelings.

He could still feel Bella as she curled herself around him on the grass as he held her in his arm. He would never forget this day. His mind jumped to her straddling him and feeling her hair in his fingers. 'Honey blonde,' she'd said when he'd asked her. He sat straight up in bed as he heard himself ask, 'what colour are your eyes?'

'Oh, my God!'

'Green,' she'd said. 'How can that be? Surely Bella and Slider can't be one and the same!' His mind went into overdrive, and suddenly he heard another voice. 'I'm Ms. Slade. I've been assigned to your case.'

"What the bloody hell is going on!" he whispered into the night. "Bella Slade? Had he finally put a name together to fit this mystery? The hair, the eyes, those unforgettable kisses, those arm touches that felt so familiar.'

"It... it... it just can't bloody well be! That's absurd! There is no way in hell that these three women could end up all being Slider! No way! No...way!" he said, putting his hands together and quickly slicing them through the air as if cutting the nonsense right out of his head. 'The first thing in the morning, he was going to talk with his driver,' he assured himself.

***

He was up early after a restless night's sleep. He was unable to get the jumbled thoughts out of his head. Sitting up, he swung his legs over the side of the bed and pushed his call button so Sampson would get the message that he was up.

"Good morning! You're up early," Sampson said, sounding cheerful.

"What's got you so chipper this morning?" Logan asked.

"It's a lovely day to be alive, Sir," he said, "the sun is shining, the birds are chirping, and nothing disastrous happened while we were sleeping. What else could we ask for?"

"Really? Sampson?" he asked, "I could ask for plenty more."

"Sorry, Sir, I wasn't thinking."

"Don't mind me, I had a ghastly night, and I'm not in the best of moods. Please don't take anything I say to heart. Have there been any updates on Preston?"

"He is feeling much better but needs a few more days in the hospital before he can be released," he explained.

"I suppose I should send him back to Hawaii for another vacation," Logan said almost to himself.

"Are you ready for your shower then?" Sampson asked while laying out pieces of clothing. "Do you have an idea of what you'd like to wear today," he asked while rummaging through his closet.

"Just a pair of khaki pants will be fine and a golf shirt, and no, I'm not ready for my shower. I'll do that later on or tonight. I have things to do today, and I need your help."

"Anything that I can do, Sir, I will."

"Ask someone from the kitchen to serve me a bit of breakfast in the library on a small table and ask the driver to come 'round, and I'll meet him there."

"Now, Sir?"

"As soon and I'm dressed and in the library, please."

Sampson rang the kitchen and gave them Logan's order. When they entered the library, his breakfast was already there, and so was Bentley.

"Good morning, Sir," greeted Bentley, "what can I do for you today?"

"Bentley, good morning to you too. Please have a seat," he said, making his way to the breakfast tray.

"You want me to sit, Sir?" Bentley asked.

"Yes, Bentley, I want to ask you about yesterday, when you took Ms. Bella home," he began. "Do you have an address? Where did you drop her off?"

"It was quite strange, Sir, if I may say so," Bentley hesitated.

"Go on, then," Logan encouraged him.

"Well, you see, the address that she gave me seemed like a ruse, Sir," Bentley said.

"Oh? Go on, please."

"I dropped her off where she'd asked, but I wanted to make sure that she was inside safely, as you'd asked Sir, but shortly afterwards, she bolted out the door, onto the sidewalk and down the street. She hailed a cab, but before I could get the car turned around, they were out of sight, and I lost them completely," he admitted.

"That is rather odd...?" Logan said more to himself than to Bentley.

"It was, Sir, very odd indeed," he agreed. "I have a confession to make, Sir,"

"Oh, and what would that be?"

"I stepped out of the car and went into the lobby of the building, Sir, and there were no familiar names listed on the board. I don't think Ms. Bella would live there, but that's just my opinion on the matter."

"What do you mean, exactly, Bentley?"

"I mean that the names listed on the board were mostly Latino names."

"Well, really Bentley, I'm not even sure what her last name is," he confessed, "but you're right, I don't think that she is Latino."

"No Sir, she didn't look it to me either, but if I may, Sir, she is quite beautiful."

"If she is who I think she is, then I would have to agree with you, Bentley."

"Have you met Ms. Bella before, Sir?" Bentley asked.

"I believe I have, but a long time ago. Yes, indeed, Bentley, she was quite beautiful."

Bentley noticed that even without his sunglasses on, Logan didn't look blind. His eyes were clear and bright, and they never wavered. They seemed to focus on where the voice was coming from, and most times, he was making eye contact with him. He found that rather eerie.

"If I may, I'd like to say something off-topic, and you may tell me that I am out of line and I will mind my business. I've known you for a long time, Sir, and I feel as if I can speak my mind freely," he said.

"Indeed, you can, Bentley. What is it?"

"Sir, I've been researching your condition, and it looks as if they are making great strides with their research, and they have had positive outcomes with their volunteers. I think, Sir, that you should consider applying for tests. It couldn't hurt, and even if it doesn't work, then you'd have lost nothing," he said, hoping he wasn't over-stepping.

"You have been busy, Bentley," he said with a sheepish grin.

"Sir, if you go through with the trials and it works, then you'll be able to do a more in-depth search for Ms. Bella and find her on your own."

"You're making a lot of sense, Bentley. Thank you for your confidence in me."

"Sir, if you want to keep this between us, I'm perfectly fine with that. If no one knows, then no one will be disappointed."

"Good point, Bentley. Why don't you apply for me and let me know what comes out of it," he asked.

"I will indeed, Sir. Thank you for listening. I've wanted to speak to you about it for some time."

"Thanks for the information on Ms. Bella, Bentley. I appreciate your honesty."

"Always, Sir," he clasped Logan's outstretched hand and gave it a solid shake.

17

It was a long three months before anything came back from the clinical trials. One, in particular, was exciting, and Bentley took it to Logan right away.

Preston showed Bentley into the library where Logan was waiting for him.

"Thank you, Preston, that'll be all for now," said Logan.

"Shall I serve tea, Sir?" asked Preston, more than a little suspicious.

"Bentley? Tea?" Logan asked.

"No, thank you," Bentley said, nodding to Preston.

After the door closed and they were alone, they both breathed a sigh of relief.

"I'm glad one of us can see!" Logan said, "I never know when the room is empty. Do you have anything worthwhile to tell me?" he asked.

"I believe I do, Sir," Bentley said, and Logan could hear the excitement in his voice.

"Do tell then!"

Bentley began reading from his notes that he found from an online search.

"A study has been conducted in Berlin, Germany. It revealed the possibility of functional eyesight restoration. A successful human trial showed stable results and that a person's vision continued to respond favourably after the treatment. Various medical therapies were studied, and they can improve blood supply by thinning the blood using hormones. Traumatic optic neuropathy refers to an acute injury of the optic nerve secondary to trauma. An indirect injury to the optic nerve typically occurs from the transmission of force to the optic canal from a blunt head injury." Bentley stopped for a breath.

"My, you have been busy. I was beginning to think there was no hope," Logan said with a grin.

"Most of what I just read applies to your injuries. From how it reads, about the night of the accident and the blunt force of the tree to your head, Sir, wasn't it that blow that affected your optic nerve?" he asked.

"Yes, yes it was," Logan agreed, "Is there more information?"

"There is so much reading material online that when I came across this, I thought it looked promising. Also, there's a great success in stem cell patches implanted behind the eyes that I saw in another article. There are hundreds of articles out there, and surely one of them should fit your needs," Bentley said, trying to sound encouraging.

"I agree, Bentley, my man, good job. Let's make a call to Germany straight away," Logan said, showing enthusiasm.

"I will make the call myself, Sir, if I have your permission."

"You sure do, and I appreciate your tenacity. If I have to sign anything, Bentley, that'll give you permission to speak on my behalf, then let me know."

"Actually, Sir, I have a permission page, for your signature, with me, if you don't mind. I want to get it signed and faxed so we can get started ASAP."

"Well then, show me where to sign, and I'll do my best to make it legible," Logan said, moving towards the table. He tapped his cane along the way, and when he got nearly there, Bentley took his arm and led him the rest of the way. He put the pen between his fingers and lowered it to the signature line on the page. "You're right there, Sir," he said and waited for Logan to scribble his doctor's signature across the line.

"From all the information that I've read, it seems that you've met with the eligibility criteria according to the clinical coordinator that I've been emailing with," he said, sounding a little bit like an excited child in a candy store. Logan laughed and slapped him on the back and said, "Let's not get ahead of ourselves here; we still have a bit of a wait."

"We'll see," Bentley said and reached for Logan's hand and shook it strongly. "I'm so glad you agreed to this, Sir. You are far too young to be blind for the rest of your life, far too young."

"Well, thank you for being so enthusiastic and optimistic. It got me in the mood for hope too, and it made sense when you said I could look for Bella myself. I certainly intend to do just that if this goes as planned."

"There is always hope, Sir. I'll let you know what I find out from Germany."

Bentley got information shortly after their meeting. The clinic wanted Logan there as soon as he could make it happen. With all the information that Bentley had sent, they were confident they could help Logan. That information brought Logan even more hope for getting his life back. It seemed like a long time since he last saw anything except black. There was a bit more light since he left the hospital. Still, he thought it might be just his imagination or from wearing his sunglasses for extended periods. He rested his eyes a lot, too, hoping it would help with the internal healing process. He was determined now to try anything to get his eyesight back. 'If for no other reason other than to look for Bella himself and see her again with his own damned eyes!' he thought.

Logan and Bentley eventually brought Preston in on their secret. Logan needed him since he was his personal valet, and he could not get along without him in his blind state. He'd never be able to travel and cope without him.

18

Several months of not being around Logan, Bella felt safe again and more relaxed. She missed her climbs up the cliff, but she had her peace of mind back, and that was worth something, even missing Logan.

Hoping that she'd covered her tracks well enough from Logan's driver, she settled back into her routine. She had Logo to consider and hoped that Logan Wellington would never find out about her son.

As his counsellor, she only knew that Logan was blind from an accident. She had no way of knowing his outcome since she'd asked to be removed from his case shortly after she'd helped him with a few exercises. She felt that he didn't need or want therapy. She'd reported that he lacked interest in talking about the accident, his condition, or his feelings. She felt it was a waste of the hospital's time. By doing this, it got her off Logan's case and away from him and her growing feelings toward him. She didn't want to be pulled up on the carpet for breaking protocol. She had to move on and forget about her emotions for yet another faceless man. It seemed as if 'blind love' had been her only options so far in her lifetime.

Her life was back to normal, she was busy, and even though she missed Logan, she couldn't see him again.

But, in Bella's case, things were only calm for a short time.

Morning sickness reared its ugly head just six weeks after her encounter with Logan on the cliff. 'How can this possibly happen twice in one lifetime?' she asked herself. She had never been on birth control and hadn't had anyone in her life since she'd been with Logo and now Logan. For ten years, she had dedicated her life to what mattered most, her son, school and her job. Not being safe as a teenager led to Logo, and now she was in the same situation by not being prepared. 'But then, why would she be prepared?' she asked herself. 'She was only going to climb a cliff? Who carries condoms on a hike?'

Her only focus was Logo, and she never thought that anyone else would ever walk into her life, especially someone who mattered. The football player mattered, but he disappeared.

'Well, it is what it is,' she thought, 'and this is what we have to work with.' She was done worrying about it and was ready to enjoy this new pregnancy. So, she spent the next several weeks, every morning, hugging the toilet bowl and trying to prepare her life for a new baby. 'Ain't life grand?' she sighed. 'How could she ever get over Logan? She already had Logo, who is his image, and now she'd have two children to remind her of him every day.' There had to be some irony in there somewhere.

Morning sickness took a toll on her. It was harsh and long. She was heading towards her twenty-eighth birthday, but this pregnancy was zapping her of strength, appetite and sleep. She was barely four months along, and she was already busting her buttons and zippers. 'This has got to be a girl,' she thought, 'Logo never gave me this much trouble.'

Living alone sucked. Bella had no one to whine to or help her like she did when carrying Logo. Her mother was a rock for her, and now she just had herself and Logo. She had to find a way to tell him, too, and she was not looking forward to that. 'How would she tell an intelligent almost eleven-year-old that she's pregnant? She had no man in her life, and Logo knew that. This was not going to be easy,' she thought.

Exhausted from a long day's work and then what seemed like endless shopping, she managed to find something that would fit her properly at nearly five months along. Arriving home, she dropped her bags at the door, and Logo greeted her, followed by Mrs. Perez.

"I'll put these bags in your room," Logo said and disappeared while Mrs. Perez sidled up to Bella.

"You'd better tell him, Mijo," she said with a concerned look. Surprised at her words, she was too shocked even to ask her what she meant. The look on her face said it all. Mrs. Perez gave her a sideways nod, with one lifted eyebrow, towards Logo's room. Like an obedient child, Bella relented.

"Goodnight, Mrs. Perez. I'll see you in the morning," she said, dreading her next move.

"You busy?" she said, poking her head inside Logo's doorway.

"No, not really. What's up?"

"What do you mean, what's up?" she asked nervously.

"Something has been on your mind for a while, Mom, so just tell me," he said, shrugging his shoulders. He looked so much like his father she could hardly bear it at times. Even though both she and Logan had blond hair and similar eyes, hers being green and blue-green, Logo had blond hair, and his eyes were blue-green. He was a miniature version of Logan Wellington.

Taking a deep inhale, she began. "Yes, Logo, I do have something to tell you. It's difficult to explain, but I must...."

"Are you pregnant?" he asked, cutting her off.

She stared into his eyes, lost for words. Blinking several times, she found her voice again. "Yes, Logo, I am pregnant, but how did you know?"

"Mom!" he said and reached down and touched her tummy. "Look at you! You have gained weight, all your clothes are too small, and you haven't looked like yourself in a while. Seriously, Mom, we learn this stuff in health class." Looking serious for a few seconds, he grinned at her, and it was like looking at Logan all over again. He had his personality down to a tee. She missed him so badly, but she knew that this was for the best. If Logan got wind of a child and wasn't serious about her, he could very well fight for custody. There was no way in hell that she'd ever let go of Logo, not for Logan or for anybody.

"I don't know what to say, Logo. I thought you'd be upset or something," she said.

"Upset? Why?" he said, lifting his shoulders to almost ear level. "I think it's cool! I mean, you and me with a baby? Won't that be great?" he said with a smile.

"Aren't you going to ask about the father?" she asked.

"No, but I'll be hoping that whoever it is, he'll be my father too," he answered.

"Logo," she said softly, pulling him into her arms. "You are such a wonderful and sweet boy. You are your father's son; there is no doubt about that. That day when I was late coming home, and you scolded me for not calling," she said, "I met your father again that day. I didn't know who he was then, but I'm almost certain that I do now, and yes, Logo, you and this baby will indeed have the same father. Please, don't ask me any questions because I don't have all the answers you need. When I figure it out, I promise we'll talk then. I love you, Logo,"

"I love you too, Mom."

19

The room was dark, with the blinds pulled shut. The doctor had invited Preston and Bentley into the room once the procedure was over and Logan was back in his room. Waiting for Logan to recover from the mild sedation, he explained that Logan's eyes had healed nicely and that they were actually in the process of bringing back his sight. Still, it would have taken a long time to get there. They were hoping to speed things up by going in and lining up what the accident had knocked off-kilter. He had drawn a diagram to show them how things went askew from the force of the blow to Logan's head. It was such a simple thing that went out of whack and had taken only a few hours to repair and realign.

"We are hoping for success!" Dr. Müller said in his thick German accent.

"That is all we can hope for," Preston said, and Bentley nodded in agreement.

"Can anyone get in on the conversation?" Logan chimed in.

"Welcome back to us, Mr. Wellington," the doctor said in his enthusiastic voice. "We have darkened up the room for the removal of the bandages, so the light does not hurt your eyes. I'm sure you've been at this point before, so, shall we begin?" he asked.

Logan didn't answer right away, so they went closer to the bedrail.

"Logan? It's Preston.... Are you ready for the bandages to come off?" he asked and touched his hand to let him know he understood his trepidation. "Bentley is here, and we will be here regardless of the outcome." Bentley reached down and squeezed his other hand to let him know he was there too.

"OK, guys, let's get this show on the road!" Logan said, trying to sound upbeat and positive.

He heard the familiar roll of a tray being pulled up with surgical tools rattling on the stainless-steel surface. 'Here we go again,' he thought, mustering up hope.

His bed cranked upwards on a slant so that he wasn't sitting straight up.

"You'll feel a touch on your temples, Logan. It's just the surgical scissors. I will make the first cut now," he said. "Just relax a little bit. There is no need to be tense," he said, tapping him on the shoulder, "you should be OK?"

Crunch, crunch, Logan heard the familiar snip, snip, and he reached out his hand into the darkness, and Preston grabbed it and held on.

"OK, that's the first step!" he said and tossed the bandage into a basin on the tray. "We are down to just the patches, and I will lift them off slowly and then clean up your eyes. The next step will be up to you. Take your time and open your eyes whenever you feel you are ready," he said and patted his shoulder again.

Preston squeezed his hand, and Logan took a deep and jagged inhale.

The doctor carefully removed the patches and began clearing the thick goop from his eyelids. Taking a dry, soft cloth, Dr. Müller patted his eyelids and cleaned away any moisture.

"Okay, open your eyes whenever you are ready," he instructed. Everyone waited for Logan to make the next move. He wanted to open his eyes so badly but was afraid to face the black world again. Mustering up enough nerve, he had to find out. His lids fluttered, and they watched, and each one held their breath. Bentley laid his hand onto Preston's shoulder and squeezed in anticipation, and Preston reached up and tapped it in return.

Opening his eyes, he moved them up towards the ceiling. He blinked and moved his eyes back and forth and then blinked again. Lowering them, it looked hazy, but it was there. The outline of someone's head was in his line of vision. Blinking again, he stared at the blank face. Slowly as the haze cleared and blinking a few more times, it began to fill in the hazy outlines. "Preston?" he said. He blinked several more times, and a cloud lifted. "Preston!" He was looking directly at him. Moving his eyes a bit farther... "Bentley?" he said, raising his hands to the top of his head in disbelief.

"Sir?" he answered, "can you see us?"

Logan was stunned for a minute and just took their faces in, not exactly concentrating on their voices. He'd regained his sight, and he needed a minute.

"Maybe he can't see us," said Preston, so he asked again. "Logan? Can you see us?"

Their faces were coming clearer with every blink, and once Logan snapped out of his shocked state, he answered, "Yes! Yes, I can see you, Preston! And you, Bentley!"

"Oh, thank God," Bentley said with a sigh of relief and raising his eyes towards the Heavens, "I knew it was possible, Sir," he said.

"I was the doubter, Bentley, not you," Logan said, "I was sure that I was doomed to blindness after...."

"That was not your fault, Logan," Preston said, cutting him off from his guilt. "You need to let that go and live your life. You've got a second chance with your sight, and your mother would want you to live your best life, my boy. So, no more talk about fault, it was nobody's fault, it was an accident, OK? Promise me that you will give up on the guilt that you've been carrying around. Maybe do something useful..., like..., oh, I don't know," he said, hunching his shoulders, "like perhaps finding Ms. Bella?" Preston said with a wink.

Moving over to the blinds, Dr. Müller opened them enough to allow a little light in, but not enough to bring pain to Logan's eyes. He lowered his lids slightly against the light, but it was tolerable. Put these on, for the time being, Mr. Wellington," he said, passing him a pair of tinted glasses, just so your eyes can adjust to the light.

Putting them on his eyes, he asked if it would be alright to get up.

"Of course!" he said. "We worked on your eyes, not your feet," he joked. He put his hand behind him to help him up.

Swinging his legs over the side of the bed, he waited for any signs of dizziness and then stood up. Preston was at his side out of habit, but Logan raised his hand to stop him. He walked over to the window and looked through the slats of the blind at the landscape before him. Looking back over at Preston and Bentley, he said, "I can't wait to get home. Pressing his lips together, he nodded his head for a few seconds and took a deep breath. He missed being home. "Thank you," he said, "both of you. Bentley, I wouldn't be here if it weren't for your ongoing research and belief that this was actually possible." Putting his hand out, Bentley pressed his hand in his and squeezed. Before he released him, Logan pulled him in for a man-hug. "Thank you, Bentley. I owe you big time."

"You don't owe me anything, Sir. I'm just really happy that this worked and that you have your life back," he said close to tears and nodding his head.

"Preston, my man," he said, reaching out to him, "you have been my rock over these long and harrowing months. I couldn't have done it without you either, thank you."

"I wouldn't be here without you, Sir. Remember, you did save my life, and blindness didn't stop you then!" Preston reminded him, "and a trip of a lifetime, to boot."

Logan put his hand out to the young Dr. Müller in a white lab coat and thanked him for restoring his eyesight. "You have no idea how grateful I am to you," he said, shaking his hand.

"I had no doubts, young man; your eyes were healed and healthy. I just lined them up for you," he said, shaking his hand vigorously. I would like for you to stay for only a few more days, maybe a week, so we can administer drops as needed and then you can go home! Sound good?" he asked in his German accent.

"I have never heard any sweeter words, Doctor," Logan told him honestly.

20

Bella

Bella had finally slipped past morning sickness and was beginning to feel like a human again. After enduring months of early morning gag sessions, she was ready for a reprieve. Now, at five months along, she found renewed energy and strength to take leisurely showers, wash, dry and style her hair again after months of messy buns, a side braid and ponytails. The new maternity clothes were stretchy and comfortable to wear without buttons popping off and zippers breaking at the most inopportune times. She felt as big as a double-decker bus already, but she was happy. Her regular visits to her OBGYN had proved that everything was on schedule, as it should be for being at the tail end of her second trimester. She'd asked Bella if she wanted an ultrasound to determine the sex of her baby, and she refused. "I already know. It's a girl," she said with determination.

"And you know that how?" she said, teasing Bella.

"Believe me, it's a girl, OK?" she said, widening her eyes and nodding her head.

***

Logan was thrilled to be home from Germany. He wasn't ordered to wear dark glasses anymore. Still, he was advised to wear regular sunglasses to avoid sun damage, especially so soon after the surgery.

He had made a decision about Preston too. He wanted him to go back to Hawaii, to the land where he was born.

He had been Logan's companion and friend since… 'well, since forever,' he thought. It was time for him to retire and spend his remaining time with friends and family on the island. It was heartbreaking to send him off knowing they'd never meet again, but Logan knew it was time.

He took his first solo walk around the property. It seemed odd without Preston by his side, but he'd hire a replacement for him and carry on with life as it was.

He'd found a new appreciation for the beauty that surrounded the castle. It had finally dawned on him that all of this belonged to him. All of it was his and the responsibility that went with it. The castle, the ground and the staff were all under his umbrella now. After his mother's death, what remained from her estate had been turned over to him. While he lived in darkness, none of it mattered, and he'd often wondered if he even wanted it. But walking around these gorgeous grounds and being able to see it all again, he knew he wanted it more than anything. Once he finds Bella, if he did, then he wanted her to share it with him. He wanted her to be his Lady Bella of Cliff Haven Castle.

He stayed pretty much close to home for the next several months under the advisement of Dr. Müller. Taking care of his eyes was critical in the weeks following the surgery. Logan knew what living in darkness was all about, and he didn't want to take any chances of ever going back there for anything. By resting, staying away from reading and letting nature take its course, his eyes had become completely healed, and the sensitivity to light had also passed. He'd protected his eyes with the utmost care. He wore sunglasses in the bright sun, used the drops when called for and rested his eyes for several hours every day.

He took regular daily walks across the field to the cliff. He didn't know why, except that perhaps he'd hoped, by some stretch of his imagination, that Bella would show up again, but she did not. Strolling across the open space, he walked to the edge of the cliff. Memories flooded him from the day Bella rescued him. Looking down at his feet, he wondered what it was that stopped him from going over the edge that day. Perhaps it was his mother's guiding hand from beyond, telling him that he'd gone far enough. Whatever the case, he was thankful to Bella for being there. Looking across the beach into the small town below, he knew that she was out there, somewhere, and he was going to find her; he'd promised himself that much.

He'd returned to his upstairs bedroom, and his life was finally returning to normal. While taking his morning showers and shampooing his hair, he wondered what to do with it all since he'd let it grow out of control. When he couldn't see it, he didn't care, and while his eyes were healing, it didn't matter, but now that he was able to focus again, a haircut was on a list of things to do.

Since enough time had passed, he thought he might enjoy a ride. Taking a last look across the horizon, he turned away and walked back across the field, and through the woods, to the castle.

Taking his keyring off the hook, he thumbed the die that he'd gotten from 'Slider' and smiled at the memories it brought. 'How brazen they were to have made love under the bleachers,' he thought. He remembered using his shoulder pads to help cover himself from being shirtless and shivering from the cold after she'd left with his jersey. He wondered if she still had that number sixteen jersey. 'Slider and Bella must be the same person,' he thought as he remembered how she felt in his arms, both times. Those sweet and addictive kisses made him tremble, and he loved how she snuggled against him. There was no better feeling in the world to him than holding her close. 'If you're out there, Bella, I will find you,' he thought with determination.

Tossing the keys up in the air, he snatched them up on their way back down and smiled to himself as his resolve found its way to his belly in a joyful flip. He was confident that he'd find her now, and this feeling was more profound than hoping for his eyesight back but with more positivity and passion.

Making his way to the garage, he decided that if he was going to find Bella, he had to be in a vehicle that didn't stick out. 'Imagine him cruising the streets in a Rolls Royce or Bentley,' he snorted at the thought.

He decided to take his beloved white Jeep Wrangler. He'd had it for years, and it was still looking like new. The roof and doors were already off, so it was just going to be him, the open air and the roll bars. Grabbing his cool aviator sunglasses off the dash, he blew a few pieces of dust off each lens and put them on. The staff kept the garage and the automobiles spotlessly clean as the inside of the house and the grounds. They'd also kept his life impeccably neat, tidy and as worry-free as possible.

'First stop, barbershop,' he thought as he backed out of the garage and remotely closed the garage door. His keychain dangled from the ignition as it always had, and he was off for his first drive since the night of the accident. The wind whipped his long hair around even worse than when he and Bella were on the cliffs since it had many more months of growth.

At the end of the driveway, he stopped and then drove slowly just a few feet up the road. Stopping his jeep, he looked into the woods and saw where he'd gone in. The broken tree they'd rescued him from was pushed off farther into the bushes. There were deep gouges of mud and grass across the ditch from his tire tracks and still visible signs of being badly scuffed up. He swallowed past the lump in his throat as he heard his mother's words again, "Slow down, Logan, we're almost there." Tears spilled out of his eyelids as he pictured her reaching for the dash. The area was deathly quiet, and not a bird was chirping. There was nothing between him and the site of the accident. Suddenly, it was as if he'd walked into a dream. He saw his mother in the middle of the road at the hood of his jeep. She smiled at him, and when he blinked the tears away to see her more clearly, she was gone. Suddenly he heard birds and saw squirrels scampering across branches, and cars were passing him. Life was moving forward, and so would he. Wiping his eyes, he pulled his stick shift down into low gear and drove off. He made a mental note to have some gardening staff clear the spot away and plant some new flowering bushes and flowers there instead of leaving it still looking like an accident site. It will be a sort of memorial for Lady Isabella of Cliff Haven Castle.

He felt like his old self as he stepped out of the barber's chair and checked the mirror. His hair was short and tailored, not buzzed or bald. He looked like Dr. Wellington again instead of Mr. Blind Guy. He slid the side of his hand along the smooth and short edges and ran his fingers up his forehead and onto the short spikes in the front. His hair was even blonder after cutting away the long shaggy lengths. Even he could see his good looks now, and he appreciated what he saw. Laying a couple of bills on the counter, he thanked the barber and left.

21

Bella was on maternity leave from work and was glad of it. Her belly was heavy, and it had dropped, indicating the baby was getting into position. To say she was uncomfortable would have been the understatement of the year. Deciding it was time to prepare, she went into her storage room to find an overnight bag to pack a few things she'd need while at the hospital. Grabbing one, she unzipped it, and her heart tumbled back in time. At the bottom of the bag was the jersey. She'd tucked it in there years ago out of sight from inquiring minds and prying eyes. Pulling it out, she automatically covered her face with it. The woodsy smell was faint, but to her surprise, it was still there. She wondered if it really was or if she just wanted it to be. Either way, she could still smell it.

"What's that?" Logo asked, coming up behind her. He startled her a bit, but she tried not to let it show. He was tall for his age, and when she turned around to face him, he saw the grip that she had on a jersey. "Mom? Are you OK?" he asked.

"Umm..., Yes, Logo, I'm fine," she answered, nodding her head.

"Then why are you so pale?" he asked with concern.

"You startled me, that's all, she said in a half-truth.

"What's up with the jersey?" he asked, reaching for it.

Possessively, she snatched it to her chest and out of his reach. He stopped and dropped his hand.

"Is that... my Dad's jersey, Mom?" he asked, squinting his eyes in question.

Tears sprung to her eyes, and hormones took the lead. She missed him so much, and holding their memories in her hands was making her crazy.

"Yes, Logo, it was his jersey," she answered honestly. But it was her jersey now, and nobody had touched it except her. It was hers. And it had been for nearly eleven years.

"May I see it, please," Logo asked softly.

Biting her bottom lip and holding back tears, she knew it was meant for him anyway, but it was difficult to let it go. Lowering it from her chest, she slowly passed it over to him. It was their moment, from her hands to his. His first instinct was to press it into his face, and the scent of his father brought tears to his eyes too. Lowering the jersey, Logo held it in one hand and wrapped his arms around his mother's expanding body. They held each other as unspoken memories lay between them. Backing away a bit, Logo looked for the bottom hem of the jersey. Separating them, he put his arms in the openings and flipped it over his head. Surprisingly, it wasn't that much too big on him. He'd sprouted up in height and had become a lanky tween before her eyes.

"Why isn't there a name on it?" he asked.

"I don't know the answer to that, Logo," she said, shaking her head. "It was his last game of the season jersey that he wore that day, and before we parted, he gave it to me. I never knew his last name. He had told me that his name was Logo, and I told him that mine was Slider. So, we didn't know who the other one was except that we went to different schools," she admitted. "Nobody ever knew about the jersey, and I've had it since our first and only encounter. I'd hidden it from my parents and you, but now you know my secret."

Logo grinned, and when she asked him what it was about, she laughed at his answer.

"So that's where you got my crazy name? Logo? Really? Mom?" he teased, causing them to crack up.

"I only had that crazy name to go by, Logo, and I needed for you to have it. You needed your father's name."

"I like my name, Mom; I'm only teasing you... I am the one and only guy ever to be called Logo," he said, rolling his eyes dramatically.

'He was so much his father's son,' she thought, 'but, no, he was not the only one.'

"Logo? How would you like to come to the park with me today?" she asked.

"I will if I can wear this jersey," he bartered.

"Seriously? You want to wear that jersey to the park?"

"Sure! It's a cool jersey, and I love it!"

"Fine!" she said, bugging her eyes at him. "You drive a hard bargain. First, though, I want to pack this bag and have it ready, so give me a few minutes."

※※※

The Park was just around the corner from her building, and she was glad that she didn't have to walk far. Her weight and the heat were her enemies right now.

Settling on a bench under a tree, she opened her iPad and scrolled to the book that she had downloaded weeks before but hadn't taken the time to read. The bench was uncomfortable and caused her some annoyances. Her back ached from the walk, or the heat, or the bulk of the baby; she wasn't sure which. She thought she might just want to call it a day and go back home. Looking over, she saw that Logo had found someone to talk to, so she figured she'd wait.

22

Logan drove into town and stopped at a drive-thru window for a pineapple-mango smoothie. Passing a bill through the window, he drove off before she gave him his change. He had no idea where he was going, but Bella lived in this town somewhere. He had to begin his search for her sometime, so he was only going to drive with no expectations for now. If he had to, then he'd drive up and down every street a hundred times.

Driving through town, he shifted his eyes to the left and right on the lookout for... what... he didn't know yet. If Bella had a car sitting in her yard, he wouldn't know the make or model. Basically, he didn't know anything about her and had no clue what to look for. Logan went up and down several streets, then veered off a side street and into a green space. Sucking slowly on his smoothie from time to time, he hoped it wouldn't cause brain freeze. The green space was nearly the size of a football field. Driving closer, he saw children's swings, monkey bars and sandboxes. 'OK, then, we have a park,' he thought. Scanning the area, he saw nothing that would interest him, so he decided to leave and look elsewhere before heading home. Glancing in his rearview mirror for traffic, he searched for a place to turn around. He was about halfway past the park when he turned around to head back down the street. Picking up speed, he glanced sideways just long enough, and he jammed on his brakes with a slight squeal. He stopped without even pulling over. Easing the jeep to the side of the road, he turned it off and got out. Slipping his keys into his pocket, he began to walk while keeping his eye on his target. 'There was no way this could be just a coincidence!' he thought. Walking up to the boys, Logan stopped across from a lanky blond-haired young man. The group of boys just looked at him, not knowing if he was a cop or what, or even what to say to this tall, clean-cut dude.

"Hey, boys," he said without removing his sunglasses.

"Hello," said Logo while the others just kicked the dirt with the toe of their runners.

Lifting his chin towards Logo, he said, "Hey there, young man, nice jersey."

"Thanks, it's pretty cool," said Logo with a proud smile.

"It is cool, but why just a number and not a name?" he asked. He knew from as far away as the street that it was the jersey he'd worn.

Hunching his shoulders, "I don't know, I asked the same question," he said, moving his head in a slight nod, but my mom doesn't know either.

"Your... mom?" he asked, his face sobering as his heart skipped a beat.

"Yeah, over there on the bench," he said, flipping his head towards her.

She wasn't that far away, but he could tell that she was absorbed in some type of device. 'Well, that can't be Bella, this woman was the size of a small SUV, that would never be his Bella, not the tiny girl he remembered or the woman on the cliff,' he thought. 'She was blonde, from what he could tell but still....'

Logan brought his attention back to the blond-haired kid, and that's when he noticed his blue-green eyes. Then like a shot to his brain, he heard the words.

"Logo! It's time to go!"

Logan snatched off his sunglasses and turned his head sideways in the direction of the voice and at the woman who had just called out. He saw her stand up. 'Oh my God!' he thought and covered his forehead with his hand in disbelief. 'She looked as if she were about to give birth!' The months flew through his head in a flash, trying to decipher the time for both occasions.

"OK, Mom," he called back. Saying goodbye, he looked up at Logan again. Making eye contact, Logo looked into the same colour eyes as his. Turning slowly, he dropped his eyes and hurried off to meet up with her. While he was running away from him, Logan saw a big number sixteen on his back. Closing his eyes, he tried to take in all of the information. All it took was a look at the boy, his age, his name, a pregnant woman months after his last encounter with her. He felt faint with the barrage of information. 'Bella!' he thought. He couldn't believe his luck at finding her on his first attempt. Putting his sunglasses back on, he started across the park. His heart pounded inside his chest as if he'd run a marathon.

Bella, anxious to get home, didn't notice anyone except Logo, and they started walking away as Logan got closer.

"Bella!?" he called out. His voice cracked a bit from his emotions. He didn't want to frighten her by walking right up to her out of nowhere, so he stopped, waited and hoped she turn around.

Bella stopped herself short at the call of her name, but she didn't turn around. Not believing that she heard a voice that she thought she'd never hear again.

"Logan?" she whispered. He didn't hear her, but Logo did.

"Mom?" he said, watching at what he figured was going on.

"No, it can't be," she whispered.

"Bella?" he said again, "please turn around," he said in the soft voice that she remembered and loved.

Turning, she laid a protective hand on her stomach and tried to make her way back to the bench.

"Bella?" he said her name again and walked closer.

"Logan?" she said, choking on the word.

He was at her side in two strides, "Bella, my darling Bella, I am so bloody happy to see you," he said, gathering her bulging body in his arms as best he could.

"Logan!" she said, collapsing in his arms. She nearly went to her knees in disbelief.

Holding her at arm's length, he took off his sunglasses and bent his knees so he could look into her eyes.

"Bella, it is you!" he said. She was the same beautiful young girl that he offered his heart to all those years ago behind the bleachers.

"You can see!" she said, reaching up to touch his eyelids, "What happened?"

"Just a trip to Germany and a bit of determination," he said, smiling at her as she looked his face over.

Drawing him close, she laid her head against his chest and closed her eyes. "Logan," she whispered.

She felt him squeeze her as tightly as he dared, and he pressed her head against his chest.

"Bella," he whispered.

Pulling away to look at him, she had to ask. "How did you figure us out?"

"The night you had left my place, I was in my bed thinking about us and places, voices, events and conversations were whirling about in my head," he said, making circles with his hands, "and suddenly the pieces all seemed to fall into place."

"Me too, that's exactly how and when I figured it out!" she said, nodding in agreement.

"It's so wonderful to see you, Logan," she said, touching his face again.

"I can say the same thing, only literally now," he said.

"Logan, how did you find me," she asked.

"I didn't find you exactly; I found my jersey!" he said, reaching for Logo.

Stepping forward, Logo reached out his hand. When he slipped it into Logan's palm and felt him squeeze, his heart was lost to this man already.

"This is your football jersey?" Logo said with a grin as big tears pooled in his eyes.

"It is, indeed, son," Logan said with a smile. He got down on his knees and drew Logo into his arms. Breaking the embrace, he took his hand again and explained to them both about the jersey. "It's the jersey I wore and gave to Bella the first time I met her. And the reason why my name wasn't put on it is that I was invited to play at the last minute. You see, I had played for the team the year before. But since the last game was so important, they needed to put a great team together, so I was an invited player and no time to have my last name put on the jersey," he told them. Reaching into his pocket, he drew out his keychain and dropped it into Bella's palm.

"You seriously kept that?" she said with a smile of remembrance.

"I seriously did! It's all I had left of you!" he exclaimed. Taking it from Bella, he turned to Logo and said, "You see, I gave your Mom my number sixteen, and she gave me hers. If you count the pips on the cube, they add up to sixteen as well. Bloody brilliant, I'd say."

"That is so cool!" Logo said. "Mom?" Logo said, reassuring himself, "you told me that the baby and I would have the same father, and you also said that this jersey was my father's, and Logan said it was his." Looking up at Logan, he said, figuring out his puzzle, "then you *are* my dad, for real,"

"I am your dad, Logo. There has only been one other person on this earth called 'Logo,' which my dad called me when I was a young boy. He was the only one who ever called me that until the night I used it, foolishly, to introduce myself to your mother."

Logo smiled up at him, and Logan thought it was like looking at himself in a mirror about twenty years ago when he was that age.

"Bella, may I drive you and Logo home? You look as if you could use a bit of a rest."

"That would be great if you don't mind. It's just around the corner."

"Wait here, and I'll get the jeep," he said, helping her to sit down.

He sprinted across the park and drove the jeep up to where Bella was waiting. Helping her into the front seat, he pulled the seatbelt across and buckled her in. Logo sat behind Logan, and he checked to make sure he was buckled up and then drove off.

"Show me where," he said, driving away from the park.

"Just go up there," she pointed, "to the first stop sign on the right, and we are just around the corner," she instructed.

"So, is it a coincidence that you live on Logan Lane?"

"Yes, it is, just shut up and drive," she said, smiling at him.

Helping her out of the jeep and into the lobby, Logo skipped ahead to press the elevator button. Bella waddled in as the doors opened. Logan got in with them, and Logo saw just how tall he was in the limited space of an elevator. His heart pumped with pride.

Logo got out of the elevator first and unlocked the door for Bella to go straight in.

"I need to lie down," she said and headed for her room with Logan in tow.

"Oh my, this baby girl is heavy!"

"It's a girl?"

"I'm pretty sure it is, and she's a mean little thing."

"How so?" he asked, laughing at her words.

"Logo was a breeze, but this little one! She is making up for it. Please turn the fan on."

He flipped the switch, and the ceiling fan began to whirl. It was on the highest speed, and things began to move on the nightstand and dresser. The drapes billowed, but she didn't care; she just needed the breeze.

"When are you due, Bella?"

"Soon, please, dear God, soon. Another week or two at the most, I think, depending on when she's planning her arrival," she said, rubbing her hand over her large stomach.

"May I?" he asked, nodding toward her hand.

Their eyes met, and she nodded. Logan sat on the side of the bed and laid his hand gently on her tummy as if it would hurt. She laid her hand on top of his and applied pressure. Moving his hand around with hers, like a mouse on a mouse pad, the baby kicked hard, and Logan's face sobered.

"Now you know my plight!" she laughed.

"That is amazing, Bella!"

"Yeah? Try six months of it on a daily basis, then we'll talk," she said, but she was joking, and he knew it.

"I'd like to take you and Logo to the castle."

"When?" she asked and crinkled her brow.

"How about dinner? I will make arrangements with Sampson."

"Tonight?"

"Why not?" he said, shrugging his shoulder. "You won't have to cook."

"Oh, I love that idea," she said, melting into submission.

"I'll ring Sampson and then go and tell Logo."

"I'll step into the shower and be right out, thank you, Logan. It'll be nice to see the castle again. Maybe this time, I won't be so nervous."

Logo was ecstatic to be going to a real castle. Bella never mentioned that his father lived in one.

"You look beautiful, Bella," Logan said when she appeared in the living room. She looked as fresh as a daisy in a tee strap pink-flowered sundress and white slip-on half-inch heeled sandals.

"Thank you. I'm ready whenever you are."

Logo had cleaned up and changed his clothes and was wearing a light blue short-sleeved shirt with navy dress pants, his best shoes and manners. He was dressed to impress, and Logan was proud of him. When Logan mentioned having dinner at the castle, and he decided to dress for the occasion.

Bella's back continued to ache, and she was edgy and uncomfortable. They were greeted kindly at the castle and what staff they did see were mannerly and friendly, or as friendly as staff were allowed to be.

Dinner was grand and elaborate for just the three in the dining room. The cooks had prepared a gourmet meal of a starter garden salad, then a chicken, roasted to a golden brown, served with baked potatoes, carrots and peas. For dessert, they were served warm apple pie with a scoop of vanilla ice cream.

Bella admitted to herself that it wasn't quite as cozy and lovely as when she had first eaten there, but this was genuine castle-style dining. And she was happy and thankful that Logan could look up and see her sitting there with him this time. Still a little shaken from the entire day and the dramatic events, she realized that Logan wasn't finished surprising her yet.

"How would you like to live here, Logo?" Logan asked. Logo was ready to jump up and high-five him when he remembered his manners.

"I would, Dad, that would be so cool," he said with a grin.

Bella shot Logan a look that he only grinned at and ignored. "Bella, how about you?" he said with a half-turn of his head, "how would you like to live here?"

Knowing he'd put her on the spot, he smiled and waited for her to answer. Logo looked across at his mother and waited for her to answer too. Looking from one to the other, she was wanted to cut her eyes at Logan, but her son was waiting for an answer that she wasn't prepared to give.

"Umm... living in a castle...," she stopped when Logan interrupted.

"No cooking, no cleaning, servants, a chauffeur, beautiful gardens and plenty of space for children to play... shall I go on?" he said, cocking an eyebrow and looking serious. She gave him a look that indicated that she wanted to stick her fork into his arm for putting her on the spot, but she smiled instead. "It sounds heavenly, Logan... but...."

"But what, Mom?" Logo insisted, ready for a debate.

"Logo..." she began and stopped short. She couldn't move, and she just stared at them both.

"Bella? Darling? Are you alright? Logan asked," you're awfully pale."

"No, actually, I'm not OK. I have to go to the hospital. My water just broke."

It was no way to get out of a conversation, but there it was.

23

Holding her daughter in her arms, she looked up to see Logan and Logo walking into the room. With a look of pride for both Bella and his brand-new daughter, Logan was over the moon. Logo went straight to his mother and pulled the baby's blanket down to get a good look at his sister.

"Mom, she is so cute. What are we naming her?"

Looking up at Logo, she smiled, then looked at Logan.

"Charli. We're naming her Charli, with an I."

Logan leaned back against the glass door and stared at her. He brought his fingers up to his lips to keep them steady.

"Bella," he said softly and walked over to her bedside. "My darling, you have absolutely no idea how much that means to me."

Logo stepped away to make room for Logan.

"I do, Logan. I've read about your family, his death, your accident and your mother's death. I also know what family means to you," she acknowledged. "I have also realized that what we had back in our teens was the real thing. I have never wanted or loved anyone as much as I've loved you over the years. Not just once, but three times, I've fallen in love with you and not knowing who you were or without even a name. Even at the hospital, I didn't know who Logan Wellington was. Still, I knew if I'd hung around too long, I would have been breaching our policy at work about our patients. I was a goner then too and then, oh my God, Logan," she said, taking his hand, "when we were up on the cliff, that was the first time I'd seen your face, but everything else was so familiar. It was like a whirlwind when I figured it out. I have missed you so badly over the years, and Logan, I need for you to know that there has never been another man in my life except you. You are and always have been my one true love." Tears rolled down her cheeks, and Logan squeezed her hand.

"Bella, I searched for you before I went off to university, but I couldn't find you. The police chased me away from the school because I had spent so many days parked out front. They likely thought I was a predator or something," he said, smiling, "but you never showed up. But my heart always belonged to you, my darling." Bending over, he kissed her on the cheek and saw that she needed to rest. "I'll take Logo home for a while, so you get some rest," he said and lovingly brushed his hand over her cheek.

"Before you go, I have to ask, how is Preston?"

"Preston is... old," he said, with a soft and sweet voice. "He came through the heart attack with flying colours. He recently helped me through the trip to Germany. In thanks, I offered him a retirement package and a one-way ticket back to Hawaii so that he could spend what time he has left with his family. He was with me for many years, and I owe him that. He put up a fuss, but I insisted that he'd worked long enough. He never really considered what he did 'work' anyway, but he gave me his all, and I appreciate and respect him for it. For his age, though, I must say, he is as fit as a fiddle, but he'll always be on medication. That's a small sacrifice to pay for a good and long life," he added.

"Well, after that fracas with him in the woods," she said, "and then learning that you're a doctor and our meal in your lovely castle... I was pretty overwhelmed. Then when you asked your driver to take me home, I panicked!" she said wide-eyed.

"I know, he mentioned that you'd given him the wrong address," he said, grinning. "Not to change the subject but, what is Charli's full name going to be?" he asked, jutting his chin out towards her.

"Charli Isabella Wellington," she said, "and although my given name is 'Isabella,' it is not for me, it for your mother."

"I love it, and I love you, and I love our family," he said close to tears.

"I don't know if I've mentioned this or not, but we have another namesake among us," she said, cocking her head to one side.

"Oh, and who is that, pray tell," he asked.

"Remember the football game?" she began. "It was played at St. Charles stadium. So, I chose Charles as Logo's middle name," she said proudly. Even though she didn't know at the time about Charles Wellington or even who Logan was. "I had the name you gave me, Logo, and a stadium name, so he is Logo Charles Slade."

"That is the most amazing story," he said as Bella yawned.

"Bella, Logo and I are going to leave you to rest, and I'll take him to the apartment for some things, and he'll stay with me while you are recuperating. When you are feeling up to it, then I have some things to discuss with you," he said.

Kissing her and Charli, he and Logo said goodnight and Logan took Logo home to the castle.

Once Bella was released with Charli, Logan talked her into recuperating with him for several days before going home.

Taking her upstairs, he said, "We've always called this, 'The Frilly Room,'" Logan told her. "It had belonged to my father's sister. I had the maids give it a thorough cleaning and had a bassinette brought in for you. I can do one better than that if you'd like a complete rest."

"And what's that?"

"We have a nursery just down the hall with a Nanny in place if you'd allow her to spoil Charli for a few days. You can walk down and see her whenever you want," he assured her.

"Logan, that sounds wonderful. I think I'll welcome the rest, thank you," she said, accepting his offer.

"May I take her down then?" he asked, picking Charli up and cradling her.

"I'll go with you, so I'll know where she is," Bella said.

"It has 'Nursery' on the door, so you can't miss it," he teased, knowing she was a little over-protective. They were met by a smiling older Nanny who greeted them and welcomed Bella to Cliff Haven Castle. Taking Charli from Logan, she reassured them of Charli's safety. If she needed Bella, she'd come to her room or ring her by intercom.

"I'll have to teach you our system, Bella, as to how we communicate with the staff," Logan offered.

"Is that necessary?" she asked uncomfortably. She wasn't the least bit comfortable ringing for servants, but when she really thought about it and the size of the castle, she realized its worth.

"The staff gets paid well for those services, and we haven't been putting them through their paces lately with only me living here," he teased.

Back in her room, Logan showed her the line-up of buttons to push for certain areas, push and hold to talk and release for an answer, and then slide the button over to cut it off. After her brief lesson in their telecommunications, Bella got back in bed, and Logan sat with her.

"You said you wanted to talk to me about something? What was it?"

"It's about Logo. I am hoping that you'll allow me to amend his birth certificate to his rightful name. Do you think he'd approve?"

"I would," Logo said from behind him. He'd walked in on their conversation, and when he heard his name mentioned, he stayed and listened. "I would like that very much... Dad."

Hearing his voice, Logan stood up and wrapped him in his arms and Logo held tightly onto his father. Backing up, Logo looked up at Logan and asked him the question he has wanted to ask for a while.

"Dad, when you change my last name, will you change my first name too?" Lowering his head, he continued, "I like my name as Logo, but can I change it, legally, to Logan as my given name but still use Logo? I know my mom would have used it if she'd known, and I want to be Logan Charles Wellington."

"Of course, we can do that, son, if it's OK with your mom. You know, those are my given names, except my mother's name is in there too. Charles Logan Merrick Wellington."

"That is so cool! Then I should keep mom's name too. Logan Charles Slade Wellington." Logo said, trying to stay settled. He wanted to jump and scream out his excitement to get it out of his system.

Logan and Bella were happy to see Logo so excited over his upcoming name change. She had already given Charli her rightful name at the hospital.

"You know what would be the cooler?" Logan said, looking at Bella.

"What could be cooler?" asked Bella, "This was a pretty cool idea, to begin with. What can top it now?"

"If you would become Mrs. Logan Wellington. Marry me, Bella, please say you will. You'd make me the happiest man alive," he said as he proceeded to get down on one knee at her bedside.

"Logan!" she said, her bottom lip quivering. She dropped her face into her hands and began to cry.

Logan got up, sat on the edge of her bed, and gathered her up in his arms. With one arm around her, he stretched out his leg and dug deep into his pocket with the other until he found it. "Bella," he continued, "I can't possibly let you go a fourth time, I'm sorry, my darling, but I can't. Would you accept my mother's engagement ring and marry me? I need you in my life. You have been in my heart for years, so you may as well, physically, be by my side until eternity. Before she answered, he slipped the ring on her finger for a perfect fit.

Looking up at him, she said the words she has longed to say, "Yes, Logan, I will marry you!"

Logo waited at the doorway for his mother's answer, and when he heard it, he backed out into the hall and fist-pumped with a loud 'yes!' before carrying on downstairs.

"You had a plan by gathering us all here, didn't you?" Bella said, smiling and dabbing at her eyes.

"I did, indeed! My biggest dream was to have you as Lady Isabella of Cliff Haven Castle. I know my mother, the first Lady Isabella, is smiling down on us and nodding her acceptance. She would have adored our perfect little family," he said with pride.

Epilogue

Bella and Logo had stayed at the castle from the day she got home from the hospital. Logan had made all the arrangements to clear her apartment and move their contents to their new home. Moving into the castle was one of Logo's happiest days. The staff had welcomed the new family, and 'Master Logo' was a breath of fresh air for them as they enjoyed having a family in the house again.

Logan and Bella said their vows at Cliff Haven Castle. In the Wellington family bible, Logan Jr. and Charli had been added to the list of names. They would forever be in their rightful places, among their ancestors. Turning the same Bible page, Logan and Isabella were listed as husband and wife of a new generation of Wellingtons.

Logo was surprised the first time a young valet showed up at his door. He was not yet used to the enormous bedroom, dressing room, and private bathroom, but now he had his own valet.

Lady Bella blushed the first morning when her Lady's Maid appeared ready to help her get ready for the day. She and Logan each had separate dressing rooms and bathrooms, and there were still scads of unused rooms in the castle.

There were endless exploration days for Logo. Between the castle, the attics, game room, the grounds and antique cars, he was a busy young man. He'd even found the cliff that his mother had spoken of so many times.

***

Life for Logan, Bella, Logo and Charli ran into a full year of happiness. It was now the Christmas season, Bella's favourite time of year. She and Logan had decided that the family would help the staff to decorate some parts of the house this year. There were huge pots of red poinsettias on tables in the grand foyer and all the rooms throughout the house. Green garland and tiny twinkling white lights adorned the banister of the grand staircase. The staff decorated the enormous tree that stood in the foyer. Logan, Bella, and Logo chose a smaller tree to decorate for their family room. It was the right size so that they could decorate it with the children. Charli was big enough to toddle around, and she loved the bright lights and shiny ornaments. She was able to reach the lower branches to hang small ornaments and tinsel.

On Christmas Eve, while the family was busy with the tree, Logan slipped out of the room for a few minutes. He came back in with a big box in his arms and told Logo that it had been sitting at the front door with his name on it. 'From Santa, it says,' winking at Bella. When Logo looked at him, Logan shrugged his shoulder as if he'd had no idea what was in the box. Sitting it on the floor, Logo got down on his knees to unwrap it. Tearing the paper off, he opened the flaps and dropped his jaws. His eyes got big and round, and his cheeks flushed. He didn't know whether to laugh or cry. At the bottom of the box, chewing on a stuffed toy, was a tiny yellow golden retriever, no bigger than the toy that was keeping him quiet. Logo reached in and lifted him out. Holding him up in the air for everyone to see, he dropped him to his chest and hugged him tightly. "I can't believe I have a dog!" he said to no one in particular. "I have a dog," he said, looking over at his mother. She bit her lip to keep the tear from coming, but it was useless. "Dad?" he said, looking at Logan.

"A boy needs a dog," he said. "It's yours, Logo. The box had your name on it, so now you must come up with a name for him. And if you want to claim him as your own, then there will be some responsibilities, but we'll discuss that later," he said, smiling at Bella, who was all but blubbering.

"Duke," Logo said, "I want to name him Duke. Since we live in a castle, he should be the Duke."

"Then 'Duke' it is!" Logan said and rubbed Logo's head.

Logo sat the dog down on the floor and went over and threw his arms around Logan. "Thanks, Dad," he whispered.

"You're welcome, son," Logan said, hugging him close. He was nearly as tall as Logan now.

Logo held the dog so Charli could pat him and become acquainted with the new furry family critter.

Logan walked up to Bella, who was drying her eyes. "Thank you for that. I had no idea you were thinking about a puppy for Logo," she said.

"I saw him being advertised at the SPCA the other day, and I couldn't leave him there. Duke will be a great companion for Logo around the house and while he's roaming the grounds.

While Logo and Charli played with Duke, Bella poured out two cups of hot chocolate and passed one to Logan. Slipping her arm around him, she nudged him towards the tree. "I have a Christmas present for you too," she said, smiling up at him.

Kissing her, he said, "You and the children are the only gifts that I will ever need, my darling." He pulled her into his arms and kissed the top of her head.

"Well, this gift, you are going to love," she said, teasing him.

"Oh? Is it by chance something frilly, sexy and red?" he asked, wiggling his eyebrows at her.

"No," she said, taking a drink from the cup. Lifting her eyes, she looked over the rim. In a low and sexy voice, she said, "but it's because of that little frilly thing that there will be another little Wellington in about seven months...

THE END

Deelightful Reading

Novels currently available on Amazon
- Gifted in Kanyon Beach
- Gypsy Heart
- The Grand Manor
- Secrets in Kanyon Ridge
- Timeless Love
- Blind Love
- The Bench
- The Room
- The Cabin at Kanyon Lake

Manufactured by Amazon.ca
Bolton, ON